SEVEN SLEEPERS **THE LOST CHRONICLES** 3

The Strange Creatures of Dr. Korbo

GILBERT MORRIS

MOODY PRESS
CHICAGO

ISBN: 0-8024-3669-2

3 5 7 9 10 8 6 4 2

Printed in the United States of America

Contents

1

A Strange New Friend

The rain poured down like a waterfall. It had drenched the small party that emerged from the jungle so that there was not a dry thread on any of them. Overhead the sky was leaden gray, and it looked as if the sun had hidden itself permanently.

The two girls struggled along side by side. The mud was sticky and thick, and each time they took a step it made a hollow, sucking noise.

Sarah Collingwood, at fifteen, was the older of the two by one year. Her glossy black hair was now soaked and hung down her back in strings. Her jaw was set; she was absolutely exhausted. Looking over at her companion, she said, "Pretty bad, isn't it?"

Abbey Roberts had hair as blonde as her friend's was black. She also had much more pride and usually took much more time with her appearance. Now as she looked down at her muddy feet and worn, stained clothing, she gritted her teeth. "Sarah, I'm going to just die if we don't get out of this pretty soon!"

Knowing that her friend was always given to overstatement, Sarah found herself able to grin. She reached over and gave Abbey a pat on the back. "You'll feel better when we get into some dry clothes."

Abbey jerked her shoulder away from Sarah's touch. She was ordinarily a rather sweet-tempered girl, but days of hardship on a mission that had failed had discouraged her.

Sarah knew that. The last mission of the Seven Sleepers had been a failure indeed.

Sighing, she looked at the line of teenagers strung out ahead of them along the muddy trail. Her eyes went first to Josh Adams, the leader. Josh was fifteen, tall and awkward. He was also shy and unsure of himself. It had come as a great shock to him when Goél, who was heading a worldwide fight against a sinister figure known as the Dark Lord, had chosen him to be the leader of the Seven Sleepers.

A nuclear war had destroyed Oldworld. But kept safe in sleep capsules, the teenagers known as the Seven Sleepers had escaped the devastation and had awakened years later. Now as Sarah trudged along, she had a sudden longing to be back in Oldworld and have things as they were.

She wanted to go up and walk beside Josh, but she saw that he was busily talking with Reb Jackson. The thing that stood out about Reb was the large cowboy hat perched on top of his blond hair. Water poured off its brim in a miniature waterfall, but he walked straight and tall as he always did.

Gregory Randolph Washington Jones was slogging along behind Reb. Nobody ever called him anything but Wash. He glanced up from time to time at Reb, his best friend. Sarah thought Wash looked as miserable as everybody else.

The other two members of the group were Dave Cooper and Jake Garfield. Sarah's gaze went to them next. At sixteen, Dave was the oldest Sleeper. He was also the most athletic and the best looking. He made quite a contrast to Jake, who was short, had red hair, and right now seemed to be eagerly talking in spite of his misery.

Reb Jackson tilted his head forward and let the water run off his hat brim. "It sure does look like Niagara Falls, doesn't it?"

"Niagara Falls is gone, Reb," Josh Adams said gloomily.

Josh was ordinarily not so short-spoken, but Reb knew the total failure of their last mission was weighing heavily upon him. Josh was sensitive and had little self-confidence as it was. Now, ever since they had failed to defeat the enemy and had to flee in disgrace, Josh had said little to anyone. Why had Goél let this happen?

Reb let more water run off his hat brim. "What's the matter with you, Josh?" He spoke with a Southern drawl that probably existed nowhere else in Nuworld. "You look like an accident going somewhere to happen."

"The accident did happen, Reb."

"Oh, we took a licking this time, but you can't let that get to you. Goél knows. He's got something in mind."

"Yes, I *can* let it get to me!" Josh said crossly. He clamped his lips together and tried to outwalk the Southerner, but Reb's legs were much longer, and he kept up with him.

"Look here, buddy," Reb said. "You know the old saying, 'Never was a horse couldn't be rode.' And the other part of it is, 'Never was a cowboy couldn't be throwed.'" He laughed aloud and shook his head. "I done proved that many a time, Josh. We got 'throwed' this time, but there's always another day."

But Josh did not smile as he usually did at Reb's words. He plodded on, keeping his head down, and a doleful expression settled over his face. He muttered, "I just can't do it anymore, Reb."

"Can't do what?"

"Can't be a leader of the Sleepers anymore."

Reb Jackson stared at him with surprise. "Well, ain't you a caution now!" he exclaimed. He reached out and poked Josh's arm with his fist. "Like I keep saying, you can't win 'em all. You've got to expect some failures along the road. But that doesn't mean you quit."

Josh just shook his head. He plodded on for some time before mumbling, "I can't be the leader anymore. I'm just not fit for the job."

Reb was disturbed by Josh's words. He himself had never given up on anything. "You think Goél made a mistake? Not a chance."

Josh didn't talk anymore, and finally Reb dropped back and fell into step with Wash. "I'm getting worried about Josh," he said.

"I'm worried about all of us," Wash grunted. His legs were much shorter than the tall Southerner's, so he had to walk faster. "You reckon we're ever gonna get out of this rain?"

"Sometime. But what worries me is that Josh has given up. He just wants to lie down and quit."

"Well, who doesn't!"

Reb grinned in spite of his misery. He pulled Wash's dripping hat down over his face. "Come on," he said. "We can't quit now. Too many miles to go."

The weary travelers stumbled on for what seemed hours. The rain poured down only intermittently now, and it was in one of those brief times of respite that Sarah called out, "Look, everybody. Isn't that a house over there?"

Jake Garfield wiped the raindrops from his face.

"Let's go see who lives there, if anybody does. Maybe they'll take us in for a while."

"I don't know," Dave said. "It doesn't look like much of a house to me."

"Anything would be better than this. At least we'll have some shelter for a while. Come on."

They sloshed toward the shack, their boots making squishy noises in the soggy ground. They had not gone far before Sarah could see that the little house was made of saplings. They had been stuck into the ground in a circle and tied together with vines. The thatched roof seemed to be made of saplings also. A chimney at the side emitted little gusts of black smoke. Obviously, someone lived here.

Reb was walking up front with Josh again. He called out, "Hello, the house! Anybody home?"

Drops of rain began to fall again, but they were all so wet it could not possibly matter. Then the door—a piece of animal hide strung over the opening—was drawn back, and one of the strangest figures Sarah had ever seen stepped outside. At first she could not make out the face, because the man had on a floppy black hat pulled down over his ears. He was very tall and very skinny. He wore colorless pants and a coat held together in front by what seemed to be pieces of sharp thorn in place of buttons.

"Hello, strangers!" The owner pushed back the hat, and Sarah could see that he was a young man. His stringy hair was brown. He had large eyes that seemed to be gray green, set in a thin face. He had a long, sharp, pointed chin and sunken cheeks. Everything about the man seemed to be long—arms, legs, fingers, nose, everything.

"Reckon there's gonna be a storm that'll blow us all away, don't you think?" he said by way of greeting.

9

"We've come a long way," Josh began. "We're very tired and—"

"And hungry," Reb put in. "Reckon you have room in your house to take us in for the night, sir?"

The man reached his long fingers upward, pulled his hat off, and clawed at his uncombed hair. "Well, I'm expecting the house to blow away if this storm gets any worse," he said mournfully, "but you might as well blow away from here as anywhere else. Come on in."

"Strange looking fellow, isn't he?" Dave muttered to Sarah. "He's nothing but skin and bones."

"If we can get out of this rain, I don't care what he looks like," she said. Sarah had reached that stage of fatigue where she could hardly talk, so she thankfully followed the strange young man inside.

By way of furniture, the "inside" had two chairs and a wooden table with an oil lamp hanging above it. To one side was a stone fireplace. In it hung a cooking pot, and from it a cheerful fire threw its yellow gleams over the small room. The ceiling went up to a point and somehow managed to give the little house a rather spacious look.

Going over to the fireplace, their host said, "You all look pretty worn out. I guess some stew would go down pretty good. Just made a big potful."

"Sure would," Jake said quickly. "We've got our own bowls."

The tall man's face was highlighted now by the glow of the fire and by the lamp that hung from one of the rafters. Sarah thought he certainly had a mournful look about him. Partly, she decided, it was the effect of his long nose and jutting chin and the deep creases beside his mouth.

"My name is Gustavian Devolutarian," he told

them. He picked up a big spoon and reached for the tin bowl that Abbey had fished out of her pack. "But if you forget it, I could always tell you again."

There were seven hungry visitors, but the cooking pot was large. He ladled out plentiful portions for them all.

Reb said, "I don't think I can handle that whole name of yours. You got anything shorter?"

"Well, you could call me Gus. It doesn't matter much. How's the stew?" He seemed surprised when everyone said it was delicious. Then he stroked his long chin. "I expect you just got nice manners. I can tell you're well-brought-up young people."

Gus brought out bread to go with the stew. Finally he brewed something that tasted vaguely like coffee. Ordinarily the Sleepers would not have been thrilled with this, but as it was, it tasted very good to them indeed.

"Now," Gus said. He pulled out a pipe and filled it with black tobacco. He lit the pipe with a coal from the fire and sent forth puffs of foul smelling smoke that wound their way heavily toward the chimney. "You folks are criminals escaping from the law, I suppose."

"Why, no!" Sarah said quickly. "Not at all. Whatever made you think a thing like that?"

"Oh, I don't know," Gus said. "Most people who come this way are in trouble some way or other."

Seeing that Josh apparently had decided not to say anything, Sarah explained that they had been on a long journey. They needed to rest somewhere, she said, before they made the rest of the trip.

"Actually, we could use a ship to continue the journey," Sarah said. "It would be a lot easier to get home if we could find one."

Gus puffed at the pipe until it glowed, then took it out of his mouth. "Might find that a little bit hard," he said. "Unless you've got a lot of gold."

"We sure don't have much of that," Josh muttered. He was sitting slumped over with his back against the wall.

Dave said, "It's too late in the day now, but tomorrow we can go try to find a shipowner who would give us some credit."

Gus said sadly, as he said most things, "Well, I wish you luck. Doesn't seem likely, though."

For all his gloom, Gus did his best for his visitors. They all had sleeping bags, and there was just room enough on the floor for everyone. Gus even managed to block off a corner with a blanket hung from the rafters to give the girls their own private room. Just before he blew out the light, he said, "In case a wild animal, such as a wolf or something, comes in, it's been good knowing you folks."

"Gloomy Gus," Abbey whispered. "I've never seen such a pessimistic fellow."

"But at least he's friendly, and he gave us something to eat," Sarah whispered back. "And a place to sleep. Maybe we can get out of here early tomorrow."

But the next day everyone was so weary that they slept until nearly noon.

When the Sleepers finally awoke, Dave saw that Gus had been out hunting. He had brought back some sort of waterfowl and was plucking off the feathers. Sarah and Josh volunteered to help him, while Dave and Jake set off for the village to look for a shipowner.

"Don't tell 'em you're friends of mine," Gus warned as they left.

12

"Why not?" Jake asked with surprise.

"The fellows in that village don't like me much."

"You too cheerful for them, Gus? Is that it?" Dave was standing behind Gus, and he winked at Reb.

"Well, it's partly that. They *are* mournful kind of folks, them folks in town. And they say I do have too much life about me. But the main thing is I'm such a good looking fellow that all the girls like me too much."

"Is that a fact, Gus?" Dave said with a straight face. "That's a real problem."

"Yes, it is." Gus was obviously totally sincere. "It's a burden all right, but us good looking folks just have to bear up with it. Try to get back as early as you can, boys. This is tornado weather. If the house isn't here, we'll be scattered out somewhere."

As they left, Dave said, "I sure hope the townspeople are a little bit more cheerful than he is."

"I doubt it." Jake frowned. "Not from what he said."

While Dave and Jake were gone, the other Sleepers spent most of the day resting. Josh was still downhearted and said he was going for a long walk beside the river. Sarah wanted to join him, but she saw that he wanted no company.

By the time the two boys got back from the village, the girls had managed to roast Gus's waterfowl. Everyone had been eagerly awaiting their return, but as soon as they stepped into the house, Sarah saw the grim expression on their faces.

"No luck, eh?" Reb asked.

Dave burst out angrily, "No luck at all! We talked to every shipowner down there, and not a one of them is willing to trust us!"

"You can't blame them much, I suppose," Sarah said. "They don't know us. We're strangers."

"So what are we going to do now?" Dave asked no one in particular.

Silence fell over the room. Everyone looked out of sorts and cross. And then an argument began as to what should be done next.

When the argument was at its peak, Gus said, "Well, I've been thinking, folks. I'd like to take a sea voyage. For my health, you know. I'm not really well. Never expected to live this long. Always heard that a sea voyage would be good for me."

"What are you trying to say, Gus?" Dave asked, sounding puzzled.

"Well, there's one captain down there that knows me pretty well. Besides, I've got a little stash of money. I can pay him, and you can pay me back when we get to where you're going."

"Gus, that's wonderful!" Sarah beamed. She went to him and took his hand and shook it warmly. "What a kind thing to do!"

Gus nodded and then smiled a rather ghastly smile. "There must be lots of ladies there that would appreciate me. I'll have to try not to be too attractive, though. That always causes trouble."

"So when can we leave?" Reb asked eagerly.

"Anytime you like. I'll have to dig up my little stash of gold, then away we go." He crossed to a cracked mirror on the wall and studied his reflection for a while. Then he nodded with satisfaction. "Yep, I'll have to uglify myself a little bit. It wouldn't do for a handsome fellow like me to be thrust on all those unsuspecting ladies over there!"

14

2

A Jonah on Board

The *Dragon* dipped down deeply into the pale green waves. Then, when it seemed the small ship would surely be swallowed up, it rose again. From time to time, Sarah and Gus, sitting in the bow, grabbed the belaying pins thrust in the side to keep from being thrown off.

"It's just like a roller coaster, isn't it?"

"Roller coaster?" Gus puzzled. "What's a roller coaster?"

Sarah did not feel up to explaining. She had suffered a touch of seasickness ever since the Sleepers, accompanied by their new friend, had set forth in this ship. Gus had done as he promised. He had produced the gold and convinced Captain Benbow to take them all to their destination.

Gus hung onto the ship until his long skinny fingers turned white. "Shouldn't wonder but we'd go down pretty soon now," he remarked. "Doesn't stand to reason that a ship like this could take much more of a beating."

"Gus, why don't you look on the bright side of things?" Sarah groaned.

"The bright side. I guess the bright side is if we all get drowned at sea. Then we won't have to worry about what happens when we get to land."

Sarah could not help but laugh at him.

Gus suddenly changed the subject. "I hope Josh gets over his seasickness quick. I never saw anybody turn green like he did."

"I know. I'm worried about him," Sarah said. She looked up at the sky then and said, "You think it's going to storm?"

That was the wrong question to ask Gus. He always thought it was going to storm. "The question is," he said sadly, "how *bad* is it going to storm?" He took off his hat, and the wind blew his lank hair. "I'd say, offhand, it's going to be a pretty bad one."

Gus's words proved to be prophetic. The Sleepers, the crew, and the captain alike all grew apprehensive as the waves grew higher and the sun was hidden for two days.

Captain Benbow stood at the wheel, talking to his first mate, a forbidding man with a sour expression. "Never seen it this bad, Asmin."

"No, Captain. Neither have I. And I've been out in all these waters. I told you it would happen, though. Remember?"

"Now don't start that superstitious nonsense, First!"

"Call it what you want," Asmin said, and his lips drew into a twisty line. "I told you it was bad luck to take these people on. I felt it in my bones right from the start."

Deep down Captain Benbow was beginning to agree with his first mate. Their passengers had not been a troublesome lot, though, he thought. No drinking. No loud noise. They kept to their cabins, only rarely coming topside even before the storm began. Now the captain's face grew troubled. "We can't keep up sail like this for long. It'll rip the sticks right out of her."

The storm continued another day and night. It was impossible to eat from a plate. The tables, which were fastened to the floor, tilted at a right angle. Nothing would stay on them.

Josh, who was stricken the worst with seasickness, could not eat anything. Sarah had taken water to him—or tea, when it had been possible to light a fire. But right now, all she could do was cling to a mess hall table as the ship rolled and tossed, indeed like a roller coaster.

"I don't know what we're going to do," Dave said soberly. "The ship surely can't take much more of this."

Reb, who hated ships anyway, said glumly, "I wish we'd never gotten on this ship. I wish we'd gone overland. It would have taken longer, but we wouldn't be in a mess like this."

Gus was not looking any too well himself, Sarah thought. His long face had turned slightly greenish.

"You see that ring?" he asked, holding up his hand. "I don't suppose I'll survive this voyage. If any of you do and have a chance, I wish you'd get it back to my old mother."

"Oh, stop it, Gus!" Jake snapped. "We'll get out of this all right."

He had no sooner spoken than suddenly the door to the mess hall opened, and the captain came in along with the first mate. Behind them were four sailors, for some reason all armed with pistols.

"What's the matter, Captain?" Gus cried out. "Is it pirates?"

"No, it's not pirates," Captain Benbow said. He bit his lip and seemed reluctant to say more.

"What is it, then, Captain? Is the ship going down?" Sarah asked in alarm.

"It's going down if we don't get rid of you people," Asmin said roughly.

17

"What can you be talking about?" Abbey cried. She looked at the sailors. "And they've got pistols in their hands. What is going on?"

"Well," Captain Benbow said and could not meet her eyes, "it's like this. We sailors tend to be a superstitious lot. Too much so, I suppose. But it comes down to it that none of us has ever seen a storm like this before."

Dave suddenly said, "Wait a minute! You're not trying to say the storm is our fault!"

"Well, it's not *our* fault!" the first mate growled. "We never had anything like this until you people got on board!"

"I'm afraid we'll have to put you out in the longboat," the captain said quietly.

"Why, you can't do that, Captain! It would be the same as murder!" Dave said with horror. His eyes were big.

"If we don't do it, all of us are going to perish in this hurricane!" Captain Benbow said. "Arguing about it won't do any good. We'll do the best we can for you. We've got the boat ready, we put food in it, and water. Now get your gear. You can take all you want. The boat's big enough to hold it."

"But we're not sailors!" Josh protested.

"Then you shouldn't have come to sea!" the first mate said coldly. "Now get a move on!"

There was no help for it. That was evident. The Sleepers saw that the captain could not be moved. When the men were gone, Dave said, "We'd better take all the gear. We're going to need it if we ever make it to land."

An hour later, the longboat was swung over the side of the *Dragon* and quickly lowered into the water, where it was immediately tossed about wildly by the wind and the waves.

As the captain cast off the lines, he said, "You'll be all right if you head east. You'll make it." Sarah thought he was trying to be kind.

"Nice of him to be so thoughtful of us," Jake growled. Then he looked up at the mast. "Do we put up sails or what?"

"Just a little one," Gus said. "Otherwise the wind would tear it right off and tear the mast off too. No doubt it will anyway."

"Are you a sailor, Gus?" Sarah asked him, hopefully.

"Oh, I've made a voyage or two. Not likely we'll survive, but we'll do the best we can until we go down and feed the sharks."

Reb glared at him but said, "Just tell us what to do. I didn't survive dragons and saber-toothed tigers to drown out in this here ocean."

Gus proved to be a rather good sailor. He knew which ropes to pull. He knew which ones to release. At last they managed to get up a small amount of sail.

"Now," Gus said as he seated himself at the tiller. "Might as well settle back. We got a little traveling to do. I only hope a whale don't come up under us and shatter the bottom."

Happily, a whale did not come up, and after a long battle with the waves, Jake looked overhead and said, "Look. There's a patch of sky!"

"And the wind's not blowing so hard, either!" Dave exclaimed. "I believe we've made it."

"Be careful about sayin' things like that," Gus called back to him. "Life isn't all sassafras and succotash, you know. Might be another typhoon coming just over there."

19

But Gus's dire warnings proved unfounded. Within an hour, the clouds had begun to break away, and feeble rays of sun began to enlighten the sea. The raging whitecaps died down into long, slow rollers, and Gus steered the longboat over them expertly.

"Do you know which way we should be going, Reb?" Sarah asked.

"Now that I can see the sun I do. We head that way, Gus. Due east."

"How far is it?" Abbey asked faintly.

"Got no idea," Gus said. "Bound to be a long way, though."

Sarah was sitting next to Josh. "We've got a chance, Josh," she told him. "We're going to be all right. Goél has seen us through again." She hesitated, then asked, "Are you feeling better now?"

"I'm not as seasick. But, Sarah, I'll tell you exactly what I told Reb earlier. I can't lead the Seven Sleepers anymore. Ever."

Sarah opened her mouth to argue, but she saw a look of determination on Josh's face and said no more.

3
Where Is Goél?

Reb licked his dry, cracked lips. He kept thinking about how good it would be to have one swallow of cool water—especially the nice cool water from the spring close to the house where he had grown up. He was aware that he was half delirious. The Sleepers had drunk nearly all their water, and all of them were suffering the torture of thirst.

Pushing his Stetson back from his eyes, Reb sat up straighter and looked around them once again, hoping to see anything other than the ocean. He scanned the horizon completely and saw not one thing but blue green water in every direction. He looked upward to where the sail hung limp. Not a breath of air was stirring. After the storm died, they had encountered what Gus called the doldrums. This simply meant no wind, and the small boat seemed glued to the surface of the water.

Carefully standing, Reb hopefully tested their fishing lines. They had no good bait, and he saw with disappointment that they still had caught absolutely nothing. Fishing was not going to work.

Reb looked over at Gus then, sitting by the tiller. His eyes were closed, and he had obviously gone to sleep. Like all the others, Gus was badly sunburned. Reb was sympathetic. His own skin was so fair that he had blistered worse than most.

"See anything out there, Reb?"

Reb turned to Jake. The redhead had opened his eyes and was looking at him questioningly.

"Not a blamed thing!" Reb's lips were so dry that it was hard for him to talk, and his tongue felt swollen. He thought of the small supply of water that they had left and knew that he could drink it all himself. It had taken discipline for them to keep from drinking it all, and Reb knew that it was mostly gloomy Gus who had advised them on that. "Better to make it last," he'd said and had rationed them all to a pint a day.

"A pint a day." Reb saw that Dave was thinking of water, too. "I sweat more than that!" He was sitting across from Jake, sunburned and obviously miserable.

Reb glanced at Sarah and Abbey. The girls were seated under a shelter that the boys had rigged for them out of an extra sail. They had fared somewhat better than the rest, being out of the direct rays of the sun. But as Reb studied them, he saw misery in Abbey's eyes and a lack of hope in Sarah's.

"It's pretty bad, Jake," he murmured. "I didn't want to say anything in front of everybody, but if we don't get some help pretty soon, I don't know what'll happen to us."

Jake was too miserable even to answer that. It seemed to be impossible for him to keep his eyes open. The burning sun reflected off the water, and he kept squinting them shut. "Wish I had a pair of good sunglasses," he muttered.

"I wish a lot of things," Dave said. "Mostly I wish we'd never got on that ship in the first place."

Wash said, "So do I. I think Goél's forgotten us this time for sure."

The day passed more slowly than any day Josh had ever known. Everyone just lay about the boat. From time to time one of them checked one of the fishing lines, but the bits of dried meat that they were using as bait had not attracted anything at all.

Josh was as miserable as the rest physically and worse off emotionally, for he still was suffering from their recent failure. "Sarah," he said one time, "if I'd just led us better, we wouldn't even be here."

"You can't know that, Josh!"

"I don't think we would. We wouldn't have been chased off in the first place. And we could have gotten home easier if we hadn't tried to go by ship. It's all my fault."

Sarah and Josh were sitting at Gus's feet, and Gus told him, "Try to look at the bright side."

Both looked up in astonishment at such a comment from their gloomy friend.

"If we don't die of sunburn," Gus went on, "we've got a good chance of living through this—unless another storm comes, of course."

"Well, I'm about ready for another storm. At least we'd get some water to drink out of it," Sarah said. She licked her cracked lips. "I know we've been in bad spots before, but this is about as bad as any."

That day passed and the night and the next day. The sun still was a pale wafer that sent its searing beams down upon them. The boat still seemed to be glued to the surface, not moving an inch.

When it came time to portion out food and water again, Gus said, "Well, time for lunch." He did not even bother to tie down the tiller. No breeze was stirring, anyway.

He took out the box that contained their food and handed each of them a piece of dried meat and a chunk of bread, hard as the boat itself.

No one was greatly interested in the food. It was tasteless and dry. But when Gus ladled out a small portion of water into each one's cup, they all watched avidly.

Abbey drank hers at once in spite of Dave's saying, "You'd better sip it, Abbey. It'll do you more good that way."

"I can't help it. I'm so thirsty." Tears came to her eyes. "And that little bit didn't even help."

"Here, you can have some of mine, Abbey," Sarah offered.

"No, I'm just selfish. Always have been."

"No more than any of the rest of us," Wash said. Then he glanced up at the sail. "What wouldn't I give to see that sail begin to flap around."

Sarah drank her water a sip at a time. She held each sip in her mouth as long as possible. At least it moistened her lips. She wanted to save some for later, but the temptation to drink it all now was too great. She finally took the last sip and savored it as if it were the best thing she had ever tasted.

"Well now, things are looking up," Gus said. "It'll be dark pretty soon and not so hot. Though likely tomorrow will be hotter than today."

Abbey moaned. "We're all going to die."

"Well, that's probably true," Gus agreed. He tried to smile. "But at least they won't have to fool around with expensive funerals for any of us."

Next morning as the sky began to turn rosy in the east, Sarah said, "Josh, you need to speak up. You need to encourage everybody."

"What could I say?"

"Remind us of what Goél has done for us in the

past. At a time like this," Sarah said, "it's important that a leader take a stand."

"I'm too dry to talk, Sarah. And I'm not a leader anymore. Now leave me alone!"

Sarah took a deep breath. Deciding to be an encourager herself, she turned to the others. "I know all of you are worried and disappointed, but we've been in bad places before."

"But Goél was with us then," Dave whispered. "Where is he now?"

"He's not unaware of us. I think he knows exactly what we're going through."

"Then why doesn't he get us out of it?" Dave argued.

"I think he will," Sarah said stoutly. "We just have to be patient and wait till it's his time to do something. He's never early, and he's never late."

"That's the way," Reb said. "You've got spunk, Sarah. We've just got to hang in there and wait for Goél. We'll make it."

Sarah had no strength to say anything else.

The torture of the new day began. As usual, the sun beat down mercilessly. They were almost too far gone to groan, and Gus went to sleep with his long body draped over the tiller.

No one talked. There was not even the splashing of the water, because there were no whitecaps. There was no breeze, either, to make the welcome hissing sound that wind sometimes makes at sea.

Sarah was lying on her back looking up at the canvas that served to shade the girls from the sun. She wanted to cry, but she knew that would do no good. She tried to think of other days when things had been better. And then she dropped off to sleep.

Some sound awakened her. Her eyes flew open at once, and she whispered, "What's that?"

"What's what?" Abbey muttered.

"That sound."

"I don't hear anything."

"I do." Sarah sat up and crawled from under their shelter. She looked at the sea. Then she looked upward, and her heart seemed to stop beating. "The sail! Look! Look at the sail!"

Her cry awakened everyone else, but it was Wash who let out the first yell. "Look at it! There's a wind stirring!"

Indeed the sail was beginning to move. Not very much, but at least it *was* moving.

"Come on, wind!" Reb cheered it on. "Let's have a big blow!"

The wind did not pick up all at once in response to Reb's cry, but it did begin to pick up. Finally there was a popping sound, and the full sail bellied out.

A cheer went up from the Sleepers, but Gus muttered, "Don't expect it will last. But it's nice to have a little breeze now."

However, the wind did last. It picked up even more, and soon the longboat was being driven across the waves at a rapid rate. And that was not all. Suddenly Wash cried, "Over there! See? There's a cloud! It looks like a rain cloud to me!"

They all watched the cloud grow larger and darker. Gradually the sky overhead darkened, and Sarah said, "Come on, rain! Pour down!"

"We'll take all you can give!" Reb yelled. He took off his hat and waved it.

Five minutes later Sarah felt something touch her

face near her eye. Reaching up, she felt the spot. It was wet. "Rain!" she whispered. "A drop of rain!"

"You're mighty right it's rain!" Reb shouted.

Now the drops were falling more steadily.

"Quick! Get everything out that will hold water," Gus said. "Don't expect it will last long, so we'll catch all we can while we can."

While everyone scrambled for cups, bowls, anything that would hold water, Jake punched a hole in the middle of the extra sail. Then he rigged it from its four corners so that, as the rain fell, it gathered on the canvas and began running in a steady stream through the hole. "Give me your cups and canteens!" he yelled. "Quick!"

Most of them were standing with their mouths open, drinking in the raindrops, but they knew that catching the rainwater was important. Within thirty minutes every vessel on the boat was filled, and so were the voyagers.

"I knew Goél wouldn't let us down," Sarah whispered. "I knew he wouldn't. He just likes to do things his own way."

They ate as the longboat was driven along swiftly by the wind. The dry food tasted much better with water to wash it down.

Darkness came on quickly, almost as if a curtain had fallen over the sky.

"Are we going to travel in the dark, Gus?" Dave asked.

"I think we'd better. No sense sittin' still. We got a star to steer by now. Though it's sure to cloud up again."

Gus kept to the tiller while the others went to sleep. He promised to wake up Dave when he got tired.

Some time later, Sarah and Dave and everybody else heard Gus when he called out, "Everybody better get up!"

"What is it, Gus, another storm?"

"No storm. Listen." Gus waited, and everyone was absolutely still.

"What *is* that?" Dave whispered.

"That's breakers, son, and big ones, it sounds like."

"What does it mean?" Josh asked.

"It means we're gonna have a shipwreck."

"Is that true, Gus, or are you just being gloomy as usual?" Sarah asked.

"Me, gloomy! Why, I don't know why you'd say that, Sarah. They often criticized me back home for being too optimistic." She could see his smile by the pale light of the moon. "We'll see some white water pretty soon, and there's no way to turn this boat around. We're running before the wind, and we're headed for land. We'll have a shipwreck for sure."

"What will happen?" Dave asked.

"Best thing is we miss the breakers and get beached."

"What's the worst thing?" Jake demanded.

"We hit the rocks, the ship tears up, and we all drown."

His words sent a chill through Sarah, but she said stoutly, "It's all right. We'll be just fine."

Wash said, "My grandmother read me a story about a shipwreck once. The ship went down, but everybody on it was saved. It was a true story."

"That's the spirit, Wash," Gus said. "Put a good face on it." He straightened up and looked ahead. "Better find something to hang onto. We'll be there in a few minutes."

The Sleepers all grabbed the sides of the longboat.

Sarah stared into the darkness beyond them. Soon she saw flashes of white water illuminated by the moon. "There it is!" she cried. "There's the beach!"

"Hang on!" Gus hollered. "Here we go!"

The waves drove the boat forward. Gus fought to keep the vessel going straight. But a line of rocks loomed ahead, and he shouted, "Look out! We're gonna hit!"

Seconds later there was a tremendous crashing sound.

"The bow's caving in!" Dave yelled.

Seawater poured in, but the boat did not start to sink. Jammed among the rocks, it did not move.

"We're caught between two rocks—which is a good thing," Gus said. "I reckon we can try wading to shore from here. Though it's probably way too deep to do that."

"But our things. We can't leave our things in the boat," Sarah argued.

Gus was insistent. "We'll go and come back when it's light. For right now, we'd better get away from here before something worse happens."

Led by Gus, they climbed out of the boat and found that the water on the beach side of the rocks was only two or three feet deep. The waves were rolling in heavily and tossed them about. But they finally reached shore and staggered up onto the narrow beach. To their left, a small stream poured into the sea. Above them, great trees shut out the stars overhead.

"Well, we made it this far," Gus announced. "Shouldn't wonder but what there are lions wandering around. We'd better stick close together tonight. If we make it through, we'll see what's to be done in the morning."

4

The Stranger in the Forest

Sarah and her friends huddled together on the beach as well as they could, waiting for dawn. By the time the first light appeared in the east, everyone was eager to see what was left of the boat. They all hurried to the edge of the surf and, sheltering their eyes, peered out to where the longboat lay captured between two black rocks.

"Looks to me like most of the boat's still there," Reb announced. "We'll have to wade out and see what can be salvaged."

As it turned out, almost everything could be salvaged. The longboat itself was shattered beyond repair, but they retrieved all of their gear, including their weapons. Each had to make two trips, and by the time they had brought in the last of their things, everyone was hungry.

Dave said, "We've got to have something to eat. Why don't we split up and look in different directions? Maybe we'll find some fruit—or maybe even some animal to bring down."

"That's a good idea." Reb nodded to Sarah. "You want to come along with me, Sarah?"

"Sure, Reb."

Carrying their weapons, Sarah and Reb headed into the heavy woods that backed up to the shore, while Gus and the other Sleepers went off in other directions.

As they walked along, Reb's eyes searched the

ground ahead and the trees above, looking for game of any kind. "I could eat just about anything with fur on it!" he exclaimed.

"I'm hungry, too, but it's so wonderful just to have fresh water again."

When they passed a spring, they stooped down to drink, then continued their hunt.

"Be nice if a deer would jump up. I could eat some venison," Reb said.

"I'd settle for something less. A rabbit—or a squirrel, even."

"Me too. You know my favorite part of the squirrel?"

"No. What is it?"

"The brains."

"The brains! You eat squirrel *brains?*"

"Oh, sure! You can eat 'em with fried eggs. Just mix 'em in. Boy, that's good eating."

"It sounds awful!"

"Just give me a chance to get some of those bushy-tailed rascals, and I'll show you what's good, Sarah."

Ten minutes later Sarah saw a movement among the trees. Quickly she drew an arrow and released it. "Got him!" she exclaimed.

They hurried ahead and saw that she had brought down a rabbit.

"Great shot, Sarah!" Reb said. "You're sure the best of us with a bow." He carried his own bow, but he looked at it rather sadly. "I got to have a bigger target than a rabbit. So you shoot 'em, and I'll carry 'em."

They had brought along a coarse sack that had been part of their supplies, and Reb put the rabbit in it. Then they continued to hunt.

Sarah killed two more rabbits, and Reb finally managed to bring down one.

"Well, we've got us some supper," he said, "but not enough."

"Maybe the others have had better luck."

Suddenly another rabbit started up. "Let me get this one, Sarah!" He had kept his arrow notched, and his left hand gripped the bow.

The trick, Sarah knew, was to shoot not where the animal was but where it was going to be. Since rabbits ran in zigzag fashion, hitting one with an arrow was often just a lucky guess. With a rifle it was a different story.

Reb was just about to release his arrow when he suddenly lowered the bow. "What in the world—"

"What *is* that thing?" Sarah gasped.

A beast the size of a large dog had leaped down from a tree and pounced upon the rabbit. It had a bushy tail and thick, reddish brown fur.

"Is it a lion?" she whispered.

"I don't know what it is. Never saw anything like it."

The furry creature had killed the rabbit with one bite at the back of its neck. Then the animal evidently heard their voices, for it reared up on its hind legs and looked toward them.

"It looks like—it looks like a giant *squirrel*," Reb said. "But look at those teeth!"

Indeed the animal was rather like a squirrel but many, many times larger. It had reddish eyes and a large mouth full of wicked looking teeth. Its red eyes seemed to glow. Abruptly it dropped the rabbit, uttered a shrill shriek, and charged across the clearing toward them.

"He's coming for us!" Reb shouted. "Shoot him, Sarah!"

Sarah drew her arrow back to full pull. The giant squirrel was coming so quickly that she knew she would not get a second shot. She also did not trust Reb's marksmanship. She waited until it was no more than twenty feet away and then released the arrow. It left the bow just as the animal reared up, and the arrow took it in the chest. The squirrel let out a piercing cry but kept coming.

Reb released his arrow. He could not miss, now that the animal was so close. The squirrel fell and lay still.

"Well, it's dead—whatever it is."

"Be careful," Sarah warned as he went closer.

"Look at these teeth! I never saw anything like it. It's got teeth like a lion—or worse."

"We've seen some pretty strange looking creatures in Nuworld, but I don't think we've seen any eighty-pound squirrels with teeth like that."

Reb shivered. "And he was so quick to be so big. A fellow wouldn't have a chance."

Sarah felt slightly sick. The squirrel's eyes were open and still had an evil look. "It's the most awful looking animal I've seen since we fought the ice wraiths," she said.

"I wonder if it's good to eat."

"Eat! Are you crazy? Eat *that* thing!"

"Well, it's just kind of a big squirrel."

"No! We're *not* eating that thing! We'll do on rabbits or anything else."

They cut the hunting trip short after bagging one more rabbit. "This ought to do it for tonight. Maybe the rest of them got a wild pig or something," Reb said. "Let's get back."

They took a slightly different pathway on the

return trip, keeping their eyes open for more giant squirrels. They also kept looking over toward the east, where there was a low-lying mountain.

"I wonder if anyone lives over that way," Sarah said.

"I don't know, and I don't know how we're going to find our way anywhere. There are bound to be people here somewhere, though."

"Maybe not," Sarah said as they trudged along. "Maybe we're on an uninhabited island."

"You sound like Gus," Reb complained. "Why don't you look on the bright side of things?"

"You're right. I ought never to complain again after all the good things that have happened to us. Goél sometimes lets real bad things happen, but he knows how to send good things too."

When Sarah and Reb reached a bluff that was impossible to climb, they started around it. "Why, look, this is a worn trail!" Sarah exclaimed. "People have been using it."

"Well, good! It's not a desert island, anyhow," Reb answered eagerly. "Let's see where it leads."

They followed the path until they came to a sharp curve. When they ducked under some vines that hung over the trail, Reb said softly, "Hold up a minute, Sarah."

"What is it?"

"Somebody's up ahead. On the ground."

"Let me see." She pushed forward to stand beside him. "Why, it's a woman!"

Indeed there was the figure of a woman lying on the trail, absolutely still.

"Do you think she's dead?" Sarah whispered.

"We'll go find out."

They approached cautiously and knelt beside the woman. She was very old, very small, with an olive complexion and white hair. By her side lay an empty container.

"She's not dead," Reb said. "You can see her breathing."

Sarah was opening her canteen. "Let's see if she'll take a drink of water. Hold her head up, Reb."

Reb lifted the old woman into a sitting position and held her while Sarah put the cup to her lips.

"Can you drink something? Are you all right?" Sarah asked.

For a moment there was no reply, and then the eyelids fluttered open. Fright came into her eyes, and she struck out feebly with a hand.

"It's all right, ma'am," Sarah said. "We mean you no harm. Are you sick?"

The woman whispered, "They will die. Someone must go—"

"Who will die? Who are you talking about?" Sarah asked.

But the old lady suddenly seemed to lose all her strength. Her eyes closed again, and she slumped in Reb's arms.

"Looks like she's passed out," he said.

"We've got to go get help."

"No. We don't have to do that. She's real small. Sarah, if you can carry my stuff and the game bag, I can carry her."

Sarah thought for a moment. "That might be best. We can't leave her out here all alone. One of those giant squirrels might get her. I'll take her pail too."

Reb gave Sarah his bow and the game bag filled with rabbits. He picked up the woman and put her on his shoulder. Reb was very strong, and the lady was small indeed. "She doesn't weigh any more than a bag of feathers," he marveled.

"We'd better get her back to camp as quickly as we can."

Sarah led the way, and Reb followed.

"Can I help you, Reb?" she asked. "Do you need to rest?"

"No, I can make it. We'd better not stop. She looks plumb sick, Sarah. I'm worried about her."

5

The Evil Dr. Korbo

By the time they reached camp, Reb was staggering. As light as the woman was, she had become quite a burden, and as soon as they burst into the camp, Sarah called, "Come here, everyone! We need you!"

Evidently the rest of the hunters were already back. Dave and Wash were roasting what looked like a small pig, but they left it at once to gather with the others around Sarah and Reb.

"Who in the world is that?" Abbey asked.

"Don't know what her name is," Reb gasped. He said, "Get something to put her on."

"Here," Abbey said. "You can put her on my blanket."

She spread out the blanket in the shade, and Reb lay his burden on it. Then he stepped back and sat down, red in the face. "Can't take this heat like I could when I was a young fellow," he panted.

"Where did you find her, Sarah?" Wash asked. He bent over to look into the face of the woman. "Looks like she's in pretty bad shape."

"We found her on a trail over that way—while we were hunting," Sarah said, pointing. "Could somebody bring some water from the stream? I'll bathe her face."

Gus ambled over to look down at the woman. "Did she say anything? Doesn't appear like she's going to make it. Too bad."

"Sh!" Sarah warned. She was afraid the old lady would hear him. She took the pan of fresh water that Abbey brought and with a cloth began bathing her face.

They all stood about. watching.

After a while Reb got his breath back. "There's something spooky about this place," he muttered, frowning.

"What do you mean, spooky?" Dave asked. "Spooky like ghosts?"

"No. Not ghosts. It's the *varmints* around here." He looked back in the direction where they had been hunting. "I never saw anything like it."

"What kind of animals did you see?" Josh asked, as though he could not imagine what would shake up Reb after having killed a dragon and a saber-toothed tiger and a T-rex.

Pulling off his Stetson, Reb mopped his brow with a brilliant red handkerchief. Then he stared around the group, and his eyes were thoughtful. "It was just before we found this lady," he said and related the incident. "We saw this critter jump out of a tree and snatch up that rabbit we were after. Killed it with one bite."

"What kind of a critter?" Jake asked.

"It's hard to say," Sarah put in then. "It was the size of a big dog. It had a bushy tail and the most awful looking teeth you ever saw. It had reddish fur, and I guess it looked pretty much like . . . like a squirrel."

"A squirrel!" Jake snorted. "Sounds more like a lion."

"It was almost big enough. I reckon it could have weighed a hundred pounds," Reb said. "And with those teeth, it could tear a fellow to bits. Sarah and I were lucky to get two arrows into it before it got to us."

"I guess we'd better keep a guard out, then," Dave said with a nervous glance back into the trees. "The rest of us didn't see anything like that."

"I'll bet it wasn't the only one, either," Reb said. "Nobody had better take off into the woods alone."

40

Sarah kept on bathing the woman's face. For some time the lady lay absolutely still, but then Sarah said, "I think she's waking up."

They all leaned forward to see.

The woman's eyelids fluttered. Then she opened her eyes and again put out her hands in fear.

"Don't worry. We're your friends," Sarah said soothingly. "Can you sit up and take something to drink?"

"Very thirsty!"

Quickly Sarah poured a cup of cold fresh water, and the woman drank it eagerly. "What's your name?" Sarah asked.

"Viona," she whispered. But she still looked frightened. "Who are you?"

"My name is Sarah. These are my friends. I know all this must be pretty scary." Sarah smiled in an effort to take away the woman's fear. "We were shipwrecked last night. That's why we're here."

"Yes. And we don't even know where we are," Dave added. "What is this place?"

"It is the Land of Dr. Korbo."

"You mean this is his ranch?" Reb asked.

"It is the Land of Dr. Korbo."

They questioned the woman, but she would not go beyond this.

"We found you lying on the trail. You probably need something to eat. Is that pig of yours done yet, Dave?"

"Just about. Probably we're all ready to eat something."

The pork proved to be stringy but good flavored. The woman who called herself Viona could not eat more than the few bites that Sarah cut up for her. It was impossible to guess her age, Sarah thought, but she was certainly not young. The white hair and the wrinkles told her that.

As they finished eating, Dave asked, "Do you think we could find this Dr. Korbo, Miss Viona?"

"No! No! You must not do that!"

Sarah was shocked at the fear that leaped into the woman's eyes. Viona began to tremble, and she put her hands in front of her face.

"There, there, don't be afraid," Sarah said. She looked around helplessly at the others. "Why are you so afraid of Dr. Korbo?"

"He is an evil man."

"Is he perhaps the ruler of this land?"

"Yes. Everyone serves him."

The Sleepers tried gently to find out more about the mysterious Dr. Korbo, but the woman apparently was terrified even to speak of him. Each time his name was mentioned, she would look around as if expecting him to come stalking out of the forest.

Then she gazed thoughtfully at the Sleepers. She said, "You must be the Sent Ones."

"What do you mean, Miss Viona?"

"You must be the Sent Ones," she repeated.

"Sent to do *what?*" Josh asked.

Josh had resigned his position of leadership, but Sarah noticed that he was leaning forward, just as fascinated as the others.

"Who sent us?" he asked.

"I do not know. I just know that you are strangers here. I have been long hoping that someone would come to help, and you have been sent."

"Well, in a way that's true," Josh said hesitantly. He looked around at the other Sleepers, then added, "We

42

serve Goél. He sends us to help others in need. Have you ever heard of him?"

"Never."

"Well, he's very strong and very good," Sarah said, when it was evident that Josh was going to say no more.

"You have been sent to save the little ones."

"What little ones?"

The exertion of talking seemed to have overcome the old lady. She closed her eyes again and appeared to fall asleep. But then she immediately opened them, showing less fear now. "You are good. I can see that. You have been sent. Yes. You have been sent."

Jake put his hands in his pockets and stared at her. "Tell us about this Dr. Korbo. If we're going to help you, we've got to know what we're getting into."

The frightened expression came back. But as Viona looked around the circle—and perhaps saw the friendliness in all the faces—she began to speak. "He— is a magician."

"You mean he does tricks?" Dave asked with astonishment.

"He is an evil magician. He . . . changes things."

"Changes what kind of things, Miss Viona?" Abbey asked quietly. "What does he change?"

"He changes animals."

"How does he change them?" Sarah asked.

"He . . . makes them different. Animals are good, but he has a place in the castle where he takes them, and he does horrible things to them. He changes them. You will see!"

A silence fell over the group, and finally Josh said, "*How* does he change them, Miss Viona? Can you give us an example?"

For a moment she did not answer, but then she said, "You know what a bat is?"

"The furry creature that flies at night," Sarah said, nodding.

"Yes. They are nice little creatures, but Dr. Korbo has made them evil. They are huge now, and they attack anything that moves after dark."

"How huge are they?" Reb asked, frowning.

"They are wider than my two arms. They are black and have very sharp teeth, and they will kill anything that moves that they find in the dark. We never go out at night. All my people are afraid to go out of their houses at night."

"So he's made a race of giant bats," Jake muttered thoughtfully. "He takes living creatures and makes changes in them. You know what that's called? It's called genetic engineering."

"Why would anybody want to make a nice little bat into a monster?" Abbey asked the woman.

"I do not know. His father and grandfather before him ruled here. They were all magicians. And now our land is filled with terrible beasts."

"Just a minute!" Reb exclaimed. "Did he make a thing that looks like a squirrel but is very big—as big as a big dog?"

"Yes, and they are deadly. They jump on our people from the trees and bite them to death. We dare not go far into the woods, or they will kill us," Viona said softly.

The woman seemed to have completely lost her fear of them, and for some time she answered their questions. But she was obviously very weak and tired. "My heart. It is not good." She put her hand on her breast and shook her head. "It is very weak, and sometimes it goes very fast."

44

The Sleepers exchanged knowing glances. Everyone knew that she was describing some kind of serious heart problem.

"Where were you going when we found you?" Sarah asked.

"Out trying to find food for the little ones."

"Who are these 'little ones' you talk about, Miss Viona?"

The woman shut her eyes, and a look of horror twisted her face. When she opened her eyes, she said, "Dr. Korbo, his father, and grandfather have done horrible things with animals and birds. And now . . ." She hesitated as if she was afraid to complete the sentence.

"What is he doing now, Miss Viona?"

"He took children from the villages. He wants to do awful things to them too!"

"How terrible!" Sarah exclaimed. "How could anyone do that?"

"He is a monster himself. Worse than any monster he has created," Viona said bitterly. "The servants of Dr. Korbo sent his men, and they took the babies away. There was great sorrow, but what could the villagers do? Then the men took me and my granddaughter to care for the babies."

"But didn't the villagers fight?" Reb asked.

"They are not men of war. We are a peaceful people. All my little ones!" she cried suddenly. "What awful things the magician will do to you."

"Where are these babies now?" Sarah asked.

Though obviously exhausted, Viona struggled to speak. "The magician was ready to begin changing the babies—so Meta and I stole them. We put them in a cart in the middle of the night, and we left the castle, and we hid them."

45

"How are you caring for them?"

"It is very hard. Meta and I cannot do it any longer. I am old, and she is young. We've been able to get goat's milk for them, but babies make noise. They cry like all babies do, and soon they will be found, and the magician will have his way."

Every one of the other Sleepers—and even Gus— looked as horrified as Sarah felt.

"We've got to do something about this!" Dave said. "This Dr. Korbo sounds like a servant of the Dark Lord to me."

The Sleepers held a quick debate about getting involved. Some said yes. Some said no. They'd had no direct word from Goél.

And then Gus said, "If it looks like you've been sent here to do a job, I reckon you'd better do it."

"What about you, Gus?" Josh asked quickly.

"Me? Well, a good looking fellow like me has to be careful. I wouldn't want my manly beauty to be spoiled." He held his head at an angle for them to behold what he considered his beautiful face. But then he shrugged his thin shoulders. "Seems to me all of us have to do the best we can for these young ones. We'll probably all get changed into giant ants. But the bright side of it is, if he does change us into something like that, we won't have to worry anymore about finding clothes to wear."

6

Eight Little Problems

Josh seemed unable to function, and Dave jumped into the position of leadership. "We have to make some kind of a stretcher to carry her on," he said, motioning toward Viona. "She obviously can't walk."

"I'll take care of that," Jake said. "Come on, Reb. Let's go cut some saplings for handles."

As the two of them disappeared, Dave moved rapidly, organizing for the journey. He divided up what was left of the roast pig so that each could carry an equal amount. He went around giving instructions quickly and efficiently.

"Josh, I expect it would be better if you would be one of the ones that carry Miss Viona."

"All right, Dave. If you say so."

Sarah watched all this with dismay. She did not like it that Dave had suddenly become the leader. She knew that somehow this was wrong. Goél had appointed Josh. But she did not try to argue the point now.

Reb and Jake soon came back with saplings trimmed, and they quickly made a litter. "All right," Reb said. "We're ready to go now, Miss Viona. We'll carry you up front, and you can show us the way."

The old lady nodded. She looked very ill and tired, and she lay utterly still under the blanket that the girls had spread over her.

They started their journey with Dave in the lead. Right behind him walked Josh and Reb, carrying the litter. The rest of the group followed, and Sarah brought

47

up the rear. "If you see anything suspicious back there, just call out, so we'll all have time to get armed," Dave urged her.

"All right, Dave." She remembered what she and Reb had seen, and she said under her breath, "I just hope we don't see any of those monster squirrels."

Viona gave instructions as they went along. After a while they came to a clearing and then followed a path that hugged the base of a steep rocky incline.

Dave all of a sudden stopped the procession. "Look at *that!*" he cried.

Everyone craned their necks. Overhead flew a huge black shape that had apparently risen out of the forest and was headed for the top of the rocks.

"That is the monster bat that drinks blood!" Viona said. "They do not usually come out in the daylight, but sometimes they do."

"Where is he going?" Dave asked.

As they watched, the creature disappeared into a black hole in the cliff.

"I bet that cave's full of them," Jake muttered.

"Let's keep going," Dave said. "Is it much farther, Miss Viona?"

"No. Not far," she said.

The little group moved onward, and then Dave stopped them again. "Hold up a minute—I hear something!"

Viona said weakly, "It is just the waterfall. We are nearly to our hiding place."

Dave motioned them forward. They came out of a clump of woods, and suddenly a waterfall was before them, cascading over a sheer face of rock.

"It's beautiful!" Sarah whispered. "It looks like a picture postcard."

"But where is the cave, Miss Viona?" Dave asked.

"It is behind the waterfall."

"How can that be?"

"There is a natural cavern. Not many people know of it," she said.

"How do you get past the water?"

"There is a narrow ledge behind the waterfall. I will have to walk. There would not be room for a stretcher. Here, help me up."

Sarah helped the old woman to her feet. "Put your arm around my shoulder," she said. "Are you sure you can walk?"

"Yes." Viona's face was pale, and her hand went to her chest in a way that told Sarah pain was there.

"We'll take it slow and easy," Sarah said.

Sarah and Viona went first, moving very slowly. She soon found that the ledge was barely wide enough for two people. But they edged past until they were behind the roaring waterfall, which thundered in her ears.

As she helped the old lady, the other Sleepers came behind, single file.

"Here is our hiding place," Viona whispered.

A large cavern had apparently been eaten out of the cliff side by water action and wind. It was probably twelve feet high and at least that wide. Inside stood a girl wearing a pale gray dress. She stared at them, eyes big.

"It's all right, Meta," Viona said, and the girl's face relaxed. "These are our friends."

"She needs to lie down," Sarah said. "My name is Sarah."

Meta came forward. She was a small young woman with black hair and liquid brown eyes. "Who are these people, Grandmother?"

"Let me lie down, child."

Sarah and the elderly woman followed Meta to the side of the cavern.

The girl said, "Here, this is her bed." She helped Sarah put her grandmother down on a bed made of leaves with an animal hide stretched over them.

"We found her fallen on the trail," Dave explained. "She's not in good health?"

"No. She is very sick."

At that moment a shrill wail jarred all the Sleepers.

"What's that?" Reb started. "I hope it's not a bat."

Sarah gave him an indignant look. "Bat, indeed! Don't you know a baby crying when you hear one?"

"Oh!" Reb said, looking rather foolish. "I forgot about that."

"Could we see the babies, Meta?" Sarah asked.

A look of hopelessness came over the girl's face. "Yes. But they are all hungry again."

"The milk . . . I couldn't get it . . ." Viona murmured.

The girl led them around a slight bend into a separate area. In the dimness, Sarah saw on the floor eight pallets with a baby on each. Meta picked up one wailing infant, but another began crying, and then all of them picked up in a chorus.

"Well, I've been to two state rodeos, a national fair, and three snake stompin's," Reb murmured, "but I ain't never seen nothing like this."

Sarah's heart went out to the babies, so small and helpless. She gathered up one. The child had its fist clenched and its eyes shut tight and was crying lustily. "There, baby," she said, "don't cry. He does sound hungry."

"Yes. They're all hungry. I must go now and get them some milk."

Gus had been standing to one side. Now he walked up to the babies and looked down. "Well, now. This is a fine thing," he said, rubbing his long skinny fingers together. "All we've got to do is to take care of eight helpless babies, a sick woman, and a girl, and keep from getting eaten alive by giant squirrels or monster bats." He grunted as if satisfied. "That ought to give a fellow character." He turned to the young woman and smiled at her. "Where do you get the milk, Miss Meta?"

"There is a herd of goats about a mile from here. We take containers and milk them. They don't seem to be wild goats, but we've never seen the owners to get their permission. And sooner or later, Dr. Korbo's men will catch us. We've been terrified of that."

Gus leaned his long self toward her, nodding. "Well, now, Miss Meta, first of all, I don't want you to get your hopes up. I know when young ladies see a handsome chap like me, they do that. So I warn you that I'm much sought after. But I want to help."

Meta gave him an unbelieving look. But then she smiled. "I will try to control myself," she said. "If you want to help us, can you milk a goat?"

"Certainly I can milk a goat. Give me the containers and tell me where to find them."

"Mostly we only have small containers," Meta said. "And not many of those . . ."

"We always carry canteens and some pans with us," Sarah told her. She looked around at the others. "Can any of the rest of you milk?"

"I can," Reb said. "We kept goats on our farm out in Texas. There's nothing to it." Reb, however, was the only Sleeper who had had any goat-milking experience. He said, "Dave, you and Jake come along with

51

Gus and me. You can hold the goats' heads while we do the milking."

It was clear that Dave did not like being ordered around. He said, "No. I'd better stay here and make sure everything's all right. Take Jake and Wash with you. They can help carry the milk back."

Reb stared hard at him and muttered something about being king of the hill, but it was under his breath.

The boys and Gus left, and Sarah and Abbey looked to the girl for directions. "What can we do until they get back with the milk, Meta?"

"They need to be changed, and the diapers need to be washed, but I'm so tired . . ."

"You go sit with your grandmother." Sarah smiled brightly. "Abbey and I will take care of this, won't we, Abbey?"

The next hour was rather trying. Abbey had never changed a diaper in her life. It was not her best experience.

Sarah, on the other hand, had baby cousins, so she'd had plenty of experience washing babies and changing them. She talked to the fussy infants and laughed and tried with little success to make them gurgle at her and forget their hunger. She said, "I love babies."

"Well, that's good," Abbey said, "because I'm certainly no good with them."

The girls rinsed the diapers in the waterfall and spread them on the rocks to dry. By that time the boys and Gus were returning with their containers of goat's milk.

Gus said, "The good news is we didn't get eaten by squirrels or attacked by bats."

"What's the bad news, Gus?"

"The bad news is that sooner or later we're going to get caught going after milk. I don't know what the penalty is for hiding babies in this country—but with a magician like Dr. Korbo around, I would expect the least they'll do to us is cut our hands off."

"Oh, don't be so gloomy, Gus. Come and see the babies, and you can all help feed them."

7

A New Leader

S arah hid a smile behind her hand. She hadn't seen such a funny sight in a long time. It was feeding time in the section reserved for the babies. The Sleepers were all gathered to help, and Sarah suppressed a giggle as she looked at the four boys attempting to carry out their duties.

Reb Jackson, perhaps, was the most comical. Reb could ride the wildest horse that ever galloped; he was an expert with a sword; he could follow a trail—indeed there seemed little this boy could not do. However, he appeared to be having difficulty feeding a baby. His face was screwed up into a scowl, and he was holding the infant as if it were a bundle of dynamite.

"So help me, I never thought it would come to this," he muttered. "I never set myself out to be a nursemaid."

Wash, sitting beside Reb, was having somewhat the same difficulty. He could not figure out how to hold the baby and feed her at the same time. Every time he took the bottle away to change positions, a piercing scream would ring out.

"I think this one's going to be some kind of an opera singer," he said. "Listen to that voice."

Dave and Josh, seated together, were trying their best. Dave had protested that he simply could not do it, but Sarah had thrust a baby into his arms and said, "Yes, you can, Dave. You're the oldest and the biggest. Now, set a good example."

Dave Cooper looked as awkward as a boy could

look. He balanced the baby on his knees, concentrated on the bottle, and seemed unable to think of a single thing to say.

Josh, on the other hand, was doing very well, she saw. He held "his" baby, a little girl, in the crook of his arm and looked fairly comfortable. His eyes met Sarah's, and she smiled. "You've done that before, Josh."

"Yep. I had a nephew. I used to take care of him when my aunt and uncle left him at our house. Like riding a bicycle, I guess. You never forget how."

As the feeding went on, Gus came in and stood grinning at the scene. "Well, you fellows have found your calling," he teased. "You can always get a job feeding babies in a nursery."

Dave scowled. "I don't need any of your smart talk, Gus. Here, take this baby."

"Nope. I've got other things to do." He walked to where Meta sat and plopped himself down beside her. "Here," he said. "Give me that baby."

Meta stared at him.

"You go see to your grandmother. I'll take care of this one."

"Why, thank you. That's very nice of you, Gus." Meta handed him the baby, got up, and left at once.

Looking after her with a rather sad expression, Gus sighed and said, "It's too bad about Meta."

"Too bad about her?" Sarah looked at him, puzzled. "She's not sick, is she?"

"Why, she's lovesick."

Sarah had to turn her head to avoid letting him see her grin. Then she straightened her face and said, "You think she's fallen for you?"

"Oh, yes. Bound to happen. Always does."

"Well, that's the way it is with you handsome people." Sarah grinned at him. "You always leave a trail of broken hearts."

Gus nodded soberly and continued feeding the baby. "Yep, I wish there was something I could do about it. Maybe I can uglify myself. I don't know how I'd go about that, though."

Sarah was always amused at Gus. He frequently complained that he was sick, but actually he was as healthy as a horse. He was suffering under the delusion that he was a very handsome man. He also was continually bringing up that young ladies followed him around in droves. She suspected that most of this was due to his vivid imagination. But as she sat watching him feed the baby, Sarah decided that Gus was a very nice fellow indeed.

When the feeding was over, they put the babies on their pallets, and all of the little ones seemed to go to sleep at once. Then they tiptoed out.

Sarah went over to see how Viona was doing. She found Meta sitting beside her, trying to get her to eat.

"How are you, Miss Viona?"

"Not too well today."

"You'll be all right, Grandmother," Meta said nervously. "Can you eat any more?"

"No. No more."

She lay down and seemed to drop off to sleep right away.

"I'm worried, Sarah. She's so weak," Meta said.

Sarah put her arm around the girl. "Yes, she is." She could think of no comfort to give. It was obvious that her grandmother was growing weaker almost by the hour.

Josh was restless. He said, "I'm going to get some more goat milk. Anybody want to go along just to get out of here?"

"I'll go," Reb said.

"Come on, Wash. Let's go with them," Jake said.

The four boys carrying their milk vessels set out through the thick woods. When they arrived at the open field, they looked around carefully before moving out of the trees.

"See anybody, Josh?" Wash asked.

"Not a soul. Sometimes I think these *must* be wild goats—except that they have bells on. I don't understand it. Well, come on."

"It's getting late. I don't want to get caught out here."

The boys quickly crossed the field, and the goats did not seem alarmed at their approach. Josh and Jake and Wash held the heads of the animals while Reb did the milking. They quickly filled the containers, and Josh rose and patted the nanny goat. "Thanks, girl. Sure appreciate this."

While on the way back, Reb said, "I still can't figure out why nobody comes to check on those goats. Somebody will sooner or later. And then we'll be in a jam."

Josh thought the same thing, but he said, "I don't know what else we can do. The babies have to have milk."

Jake said, "Maybe we can capture a wild goat and keep it in the cave."

"Jake, you're always full of schemes," Reb said. "Who wants to live with a goat?"

The two argued until they got back to the waterfall. They followed the narrow ledge, then stepped inside the cave.

Sarah and Meta came to meet them. "We'll take the milk," Sarah said. "And thanks. By the way, we're having rabbit for supper."

"Again!" Wash moaned. "I think I can feel my ears growing. I'm going to turn into a rabbit."

"I hadn't noticed you turning down any," Gus said. He was already sitting by the fire at the cave entrance, grilling rabbits on spits. When the boys joined him, he said, "Just half a rabbit apiece tonight. Hunting wasn't too good."

"We can always eat one of the goats," Dave grumbled.

"Why, we couldn't do that," Josh said, shocked. "They're not ours!"

"So what! The milk we're taking isn't ours, either."

"But that's not for us!" Josh argued. "That's for the babies."

"I don't want to argue, Josh. I'm tired of babies, and I'm tired of goats. I think we ought to get out of here."

"Nothing I'd like better," Josh said, "but we have responsibilities."

Dave looked sourly at him. "Then why don't you think of a way to take care of the responsibilities *and* get us all out of here?"

Josh dropped his head. He knew that Dave was unhappy with him. He was unhappy with himself, but he could think of no good reply.

They ate supper, which included a salad made from some leafy plants that Gus had brought in. He had found some berries too—not many but enough for everyone to have a taste.

After the babies were put down for the night, everyone sat around the main room of the cave.

"Now it's time for a war council," Dave said.

He had been planning this, Josh realized, ever since their confrontation. Josh just sat there, knowing what was coming.

"I've been talking to Meta, and she tells me that there's a way to get out of the Land of Dr. Korbo without going by ship. Isn't that right, Meta?"

"There is a way, but it is very dangerous."

"Tell them about it, Meta," Dave said. He was staring at Josh, challenging him without a word.

"There's a way through the forest, but that part of the Land of Dr. Korbo is filled with monsters that he has made. Many of our villagers have lost their lives there."

"But most weren't archers like we are, and they can't use swords," Dave argued. "We could fight our way through."

"How far is it?" Reb asked.

"That I do not know."

"Well, what's on the other side of the forest when we get there?" Jake asked.

"I have never been there. There was one man who went and came back. He said that Korbo has no power on the other side of the mountains."

"Why would the man come back to this terrible place?" Josh asked.

"I don't know. Some say he never really went. That he just stayed in the woods and came back with made-up lies."

"Still, we've got to try it," Dave said. He looked at Josh again and said, "Last chance, Josh. Are you going to lead or not?"

Josh lowered his head, then got to his feet. He looked around miserably and then shook his head. "I can't handle it, Dave." He turned and walked toward the cave entrance.

Sarah jumped up. "Josh, wait a minute!"

Dave said, "Sarah, come back!"

***

Sarah paid Dave no heed. She hurried to catch up with Josh, who was already making his way out from under the waterfall. She caught him just as they came clear of it. "You can't be out here, Josh! Not at night. Those bats are out after dark."

"I don't care, Sarah. I wouldn't care if a bat did get me!"

"Come back inside, Josh. You've got to take a leadership role."

"Why should I?"

"Because Goél's commanded you to lead us, that's why. You're unfaithful to him when you give up."

"He doesn't know about my failure."

"Of course, he knows. *How* he knows these things, I don't know. But you know he's proved a hundred times that he knows what's going on."

"Well, I can't help it! I just feel rotten. I wish I had never gotten into that stupid sleep capsule. I wish I had stayed back in Oldworld when it blew up."

"You don't mean that!"

"Well, maybe not . . . but I can't lead anymore. That's all there is to it."

Sarah began talking earnestly. She and Josh had been best friends even before they had awakened in Nuworld and emerged from their sleep capsules.

"Think about what Goél's done for us in the past. He's let us be in some awful places, but he's always sent help at just the right time. That's the way Goél does things. And he uses people. And he's chosen you to be our leader."

Josh still hesitated. "I'd like to, Sarah," he groaned. "I really would. But I just don't feel like leading anymore!"

"Then you've got to lead whether you feel like it or not."

"How do you do that?"

"I've had to do things I didn't want to do lots of times," Sarah said. The thunder of the waterfall over their heads made it hard to talk, so she moved closer and shouted in Josh's ear. "You just do it whether you want to or not. Goél's given us a job, and we've got to do it. *You've* got to do it, Josh!"

Sarah pleaded for a long time, and Josh finally said with a sigh, "All right, Sarah. I'll try it, but I don't know how well I'll do."

"Wonderful! Come on. Let's go back to the meeting."

They went back into the cave and found the others waiting for them.

"Well, we're leaving tomorrow morning," Dave announced.

Josh said, "Hold on a minute, Dave. There's a little more to it than that."

"It's already decided, Josh. You had your chance."

"Wait a minute!" Josh argued, his voice growing louder. "We've got a sick woman here and eight babies. What about them?"

"I'll take care of all that. We'll be all right."

Sarah waited for Josh to assert himself further. Then, with a sinking heart, she saw that he was not going to. He simply sat and stared into the fire.

"That's it," Dave said firmly. "We leave at first light."

Sometime during the night, Sarah heard a muffled sound. She got out of her blanket and made her way to the other side of the cavern. There she found Meta kneeling beside her grandmother and weeping.

62

"What is it, Meta? Is she worse?"

Meta whispered, "She's died, Sarah."

When Sarah knelt beside the girl, Meta turned and fell into her arms. She felt Meta's shoulders shaking with her weeping.

"It's all right, Meta. She called us the Sent Ones— and I believe we were sent here to help you. Your grandmother is gone, but we're still here. And we'll be your friends."

8

Goat Rustlers

Sarah stood beside Meta as the boys filled in the grave. She heard the girl whisper, "I'll miss her so much. But I am so thankful you are here."

As soon as the burial was over, Dave said, "It's time to pull out."

"What are we going to do about these babies?" Josh ventured.

"We're going to carry them. There are eight of them, and there are nine of us, so we'll make it."

They quickly gathered their gear together, but when Dave said, "Let's go," Reb held up a hand. "We're not ready to leave yet."

As usual, Dave didn't like to have his decisions questioned. "Look, Reb, we've got to get on our way. We've got to make time."

But Reb shook his head. "What are you planning to *feed* these babies, Dave?"

Dave opened his mouth to speak. He probably was about to say, "Goat's milk," but then realized what Reb was driving at. He said rather feebly, "Well, there'll probably be other goats along the way."

"We can't be sure of that," Reb said. "I'm going to play it safe. I'm going to take along something for those kids to eat."

"So what are you going to do, Reb?" Wash had a worried look on his face.

Reb Jackson said, "I always despised horse

thieves and cattle rustlers, but I guess I'm gonna have to join their ranks."

"What do you mean?" Jake asked.

"I mean we've got to get some of those goats and take 'em with us. We don't know how long we'll be on the trail, and we can't depend on finding any milk on the way. There ain't no supermarkets out here, you know, Dave."

"Wait a minute, yourself," Dave said. "Those are not our goats!"

"That's what I'm telling you, Dave. I'm gonna rustle 'em."

A lively argument took place then. Some agreed with Reb that they would have to have fresh milk, but nobody really wanted to steal the goats.

At last Sarah said, "I know what we can do."

"What?" Abbey asked.

"We can leave payment for the goats—and for the milk we've taken, too."

Reb turned to Meta. "What kind of money do people use here, Meta?"

"People here do not use money. We trade."

Sarah said excitedly, "All right, then. Let's go through our things and find enough stuff to leave that would be the equivalent of—how many goats will we need?"

"I figure four," Reb said. "Just to be on the safe side."

"Meta, you do it. Take enough of our things to equal the value of four goats and all the milk."

Meta hesitated, but at Sarah's urging she finally said, "All right."

The Sleepers and Gus spread out their equipment. Meta went through everything and made her choices.

Only Dave protested. "They can't have my magnifying glass! I can use it to start a fire!"

"Let her have it, Dave. We'll start a fire with flint

and steel," Sarah said. "Anything to make the payment right."

In the end, Reb took the items that Meta had selected and tied them up in a cloth. He put his bright red handkerchief at the top so that the bundle would be easily seen. Then he said, "I'll go to the clearing and leave this stuff. Which way you going, Dave?"

"That way." Dave pointed. "Meta says the pass is through the mountains."

"Then you take on off," Reb said.

"What about you?" Sarah asked. "How will you find us?"

"If I couldn't track a bunch like this, I'd take down my sign!" Reb snorted. "Now get going. I'll catch up sooner or later."

"I'd better stay with you, Reb," Gus said.

"All right. I could use a little help. You could lead two of the critters. Let's go, Gus."

Reb and Gus hiked through the woods to where the goats were. "Still don't see anybody around. Where should we leave this stuff?" Reb asked.

"I guess somewhere where the goats can't get at it and eat it. What about we hang it from the limb of that tree? The owners can't miss it there."

"You think they'll figure out what happened?"

"They'll probably take the stuff and then send somebody out to arrest us anyway." But Gus grinned.

"Aw, you're no help. Let's pick out the four best milkers."

They selected four nannies, and Reb used pieces of the lasso he had cut up to make a lead rope for each goat. "You take these two, and I'll lead this pair."

"This was a good idea you had, Reb. I had bad feelings about starting out with those babies and nothing for them to eat."

They started back across the open field with the goats. They had almost reached the trees when suddenly Gus hollered, "Look out, Reb!"

Reb looked up to see a terrifying sight. He had seen beetles before. He had even played with them when he was small. He especially liked the black beetles with the big pincers on their heads.

But the beetle that was coming at them from among the trees was enormous!

"Here," Reb said quickly. "You hang onto all these goats."

"What are you going to do?"

"I'm gonna discourage that bug."

Reb drew his sword and ran straight toward the beetle. Balanced on long bent legs, it loomed over Reb's head. It had shiny black eyes, and its pincers looked big enough to cut him in two. The pincers made a clicking sound as it advanced.

"Come on, you varmint!" Reb said, swishing his sword. "Let's see who's going to come out of this on top!"

The giant beetle was not fast, but there was something frightening about the steady *click click click* of the great pincers. They were sharp and serrated, and Reb knew he was lost if the beetle ever got hold of him.

"Run, Reb!" Gus said. "Don't try to fight that thing! He'll kill you!"

But Reb Jackson loved a fight. He also was fairly sure that the beetle was coming for the goats, not for him or Gus. The insect wasn't equipped to protect itself against a sword. "Don't worry," he said.

But then he saw the wicked pincers head for him,

and he leaped to one side just as they came together with a vicious *click*. Quickly Reb slashed with his sword and severed one of the creature's front legs.

A leg might be gone, but the beetle still had wicked pincers that could kill. Reb dodged around as it lumbered after him on five legs. The pincers closed on the sleeve of his shirt, tearing it free. But at the same time Reb leaped forward and severed another leg. The beetle pitched forward.

"You got him now, Reb! Whittle him down to size!"

Reb danced around, and the beetle could not move fast enough now. With a mighty blow he severed the head.

Panting, he looked at the great insect. "If they ever need a bug exterminator in this place, I guess I'm elected." He sheathed his sword and took the leads of his two goats. "And I guess we'd better mosey on."

"How do you *mosey?*"

"That means walk."

"Oh!" Gus cast him an admiring glance. "You know, you're not as good looking as I am, but you sure are good with that sword. We'll probably need it when we meet up with the rest of Korbo's monsters. That big beetle, he's probably just nothing compared to what's waiting for us in that forest."

"You sure know how to cheer a fellow up, Gus."

"Oh, yes. Everybody says that. Back at home they always said I was too full of fun and joy."

As they trudged on, Reb said, "Don't tell 'em about that big bug. It'd just worry the girls."

"I thought it'd make a good story."

"No," Reb said. "We don't need any more stories. We've got enough real monsters ahead of us."

9
Danger at the River

The unusual parade that wound through the forest would have startled any of the inhabitants. In the lead was Dave Cooper, the only one not bearing a bundle containing a baby. He ranged on ahead, and his eyes constantly checked out the path. From time to time he looked up into the trees as well.

He was immediately followed by Meta. She was carrying all she could on her back, as were the rest of the party. In her arms she cradled a small infant. Now and then Dave would turn and speak to her, and she would point ahead, saying, "That way. We keep going that way."

Arranged behind these two were the other six Sleepers, each carrying a baby. The rear was brought up by a lanky figure wearing a floppy hat. Every once in a while Gus made a pessimistic remark. But then he would look down at the solemn face of the baby in his arm and say something like, "Well, now, miss, it's a good thing you're just a baby. If you were a few years older, you'd be bound to fall in love with me."

Sarah, who was next to last in line, right in front of Gus, smiled when she heard his last such comment. But then she sighed and returned to worrying about Josh. He had said little since he had given up trying to assert his leadership. Still, *she* had not given up, and every time they stopped to rest she would sit beside him and try to say something encouraging.

71

**

Reb plodded along, carrying the baby assigned to him. The four goats were strung out in a line behind him. The animals followed along patiently, bleating piteously sometimes.

The travelers took a break at midmorning. Reb and Gus milked the goats just enough to provide a quick meal for the babies. They drank it happily and went to sleep almost at once.

"It's a good thing these babies sleep a lot," Reb muttered. "If they all decided to squall at once, we'd sure attract some attention."

Wash was leaning back against a tree. Like the others, he'd been watching for monsters overhead during their rest period. "I sure hope we don't see any of those squirrels," he said.

"Oh, we're bound to see a few." Gus was sitting on the ground across from Wash. He glanced upward and added, "Can't expect to make an omelet without breaking a few eggs, you know."

"What in the world does *that* mean?" Jake asked.

"It means that on a good adventure like this we're bound to have a few bad things happen. But that's all right. My theory is that bad things make a fellow tough."

"I'm tough enough already," Jake growled. "Don't be coming at me with any of your dark prophecies! My lands, Gus, don't you ever have any optimistic thoughts?"

Gus looked surprised. "Why, sure I do. I expect I'll get married someday and live happily ever after. But that's after I've gone through a lot of hard stuff."

"I give up!" Reb said in disgust. He began to pet

one of the goats, saying, "You're a lot more cheerful than Gus is, Mrs. Goat."

Josh was still not fully rested when Dave said, "Let's get started."

Josh looked up. "It wouldn't hurt to take another ten minutes. Everybody's tired."

Dave shook his head. "I say it's time to go. Josh, you had your chance to be a leader and tell us what to do. Now let's see you be a follower."

A hot reply came to Josh's lips, but he bit it back, thinking, *I guess he's right.* He noticed Sarah staring at him strangely, and he avoided her glance.

They stopped again at noon, took care of the babies, and ate some dried meat that had become hard and tasteless.

At midafternoon they were passing through a level open spot when Gus said with obvious pleasure, "Would you look at that over there."

"Look at what?" Dave asked.

"That's wild grain growing over there. And it's ripe."

"So what?" Dave said. "Keep moving."

"Hold up just a minute." Gus stood holding his baby in one arm and looking thoughtfully at the yellow grain. "Let's take a break here. I'd like to try some-thing."

"We don't have time for any more breaks."

Ignoring Dave, Reb said, "What's on your mind, Gus?"

"That grain out there is pretty sorry stuff, but we could harvest it. See—the heads on it are fully grown."

Josh walked over to the grain and plucked a handful. "You're right. It's ready. But what could we do with it?"

"We could pick enough of it to make some kind of meal. We could crunch it up."

"We don't have *time* for that, Gus!" Dave growled. "Let's go!"

"We could use a little something besides milk and dried meat," Gus suggested. "We could crush it maybe and make something like flour or cornmeal. And then we could cook some mush."

"Oh, that would be wonderful!" Meta said with a broad smile. "The babies need something besides milk, too. What a smart man you are!"

Gus glanced at Meta. She was beaming at him. "Well, I suppose you're right about that. Anyway, I don't know much about babies, but I could use a little mush myself."

Dave still argued against stopping, but everyone was tired. Meta and Abbey cared for the babies while the rest went to gather a harvest of the wild grain.

Jake found a large flat rock with a hollow in it. Then he went looking for one that would just about fit into the hollow place. He came back wearing a big smile. "Let's try this out," he said.

He poured some grain into the hollow place, then began pushing down on it with the smaller stone. He turned the small stone around and around. After doing this awhile, he took it away and grinned. "See. Cornmeal."

"Hey, that's great!" Wash said. "I'll get a fire started, and we can have mush and milk."

They took turns grinding grain until they had ground enough to make mush for everyone.

While this was going on, Gus wandered off and came back with some roots. "These are almost like sweet potatoes," he said. "I eat them all the time."

It was a cheerful time for all when they sat down to hot mush and sweet potatoes.

"We'll try to bring down a deer or something when we can," Reb said, "but this goes down mighty well."

Josh had become very attached to the baby he carried, although he would not have admitted it. Her name, Meta told him, was Susan. He chuckled as he fed her spoonfuls of mush, for she would swallow some and the rest would just come leaking out. He became expert at catching it with a spoon and shoveling it back in again.

Sarah was watching him with a smile. Her own infant, a boy named Bobby, had already gone to sleep. "Susan is a slow eater," she said.

"Susie just enjoys her food." Josh continued to spoon in the mush, saying, "She's a good baby. Probably the best of all of them."

"You're just proud of her because she's yours."

"I guess so. Funny how we tend to think things like that." He studied the baby's face and saw that she was getting sleepy. He fed her the rest of her mush and then put her on his shoulder. He patted her back until eventually he was rewarded with a thunderous burp.

"You do that so well. You'll be a wonderful father." Sarah smiled shyly at him. "A wonderful husband too."

Josh stared at her blankly, wondering where that idea came from. Then he automatically looked up into the trees again. "I'm glad we haven't been attacked by any of those giant squirrels or any bats. But I have to say I'm worried about tonight—sleeping out in the open. Those bats could come down on us at any time. Miss Viona said they fly even in the daylight sometimes."

"You ought to see to it that we stop early and find

some kind of shelter. Maybe another cave," Sarah told him.

"Dave wouldn't like that. He's the leader now."

"Well, I keep telling you, Josh, that you need to speak up."

"It's too late for that."

"It's never too late to start doing what you're supposed to be doing. We ought to start looking for a place right now. Go tell Dave."

Josh hesitated but then shrugged his shoulders. "All right," he said doubtfully. "I'll try."

He put Susie down with the other babies, and Sarah did the same with Bobby. Leaving all the infants in Meta's care, the two walked over to the riverside where Gus and the other boys were fishing.

"Hey, you want me to cut you a pole, Sarah?" Reb asked. "They're biting good." He pulled up a stringer of silvery fish. "Look at these beauties. We're going to have fish for supper tonight. I sure wish we had some onions to make onion rings with and some real cornmeal for hush puppies."

Gus, who was fishing off to one side, glanced over at Reb, and a frown wrinkled his long face. "What's *hush puppies?*"

"Oh, they're little round pieces of cornbread, Gus. My mom used to make 'em. When one of the dogs would start barking and begging, she would throw him one and say, 'Hush, puppy.'"

"I don't need a pole, Reb," Sarah said. "I'll just watch you boys fish. But thanks." She looked over at Josh then and nodded her head toward Dave.

Taking the hint, Josh said, "Dave, don't you think we'd better start trying to find some shelter?"

"We've got plenty of time for that," Dave said carelessly.

"But I'm worried about us being out after dark. Those bats . . ."

"You worry about too many things, Josh. Cut yourself a pole and start fishing."

Desperately Josh said, "Dave, you've seen one of those bats. Imagine what would happen if a whole bunch of them came down on us at once. And that could happen if we're out in the open."

Sarah put in quickly, "He's right, you know. We must get into a safe place before dark."

But Dave shook his head. "I'll look around for a safe place after we catch a few more fish. Why don't you start cleaning these we've caught, Josh?"

Josh grew angry then, but he had no time to express his annoyance.

"I got me a big one!" Wash cried. He struggled with his pole as the fishing line zipped around in the water. "I can't pull him in, he's so big!"

Josh yelled advice. Everybody began yelling advice.

With great effort Wash managed to pull back his pole. It bent, but out of the water came a beautiful fat fish, far bigger than any the other boys had caught.

"That's a great one. Hang onto him!" Reb yelled. "Pull him up higher. I'll go out and get him. You'll never land him."

Reb put down his own pole and stepped into the water. But he had gotten in no deeper than his knees when suddenly something burst out of the depths of the river.

Things happened so quickly that no one had time to react. First, Josh saw this huge pale creature emerge. Its body was alligatorlike. It had fangs like a serpent and luminous round eyes and a mouthful of sharp teeth. It shot up out of the water, and in an instant Wash's beautiful big fish had disappeared down its gullet. As the creature fell back into the river, its teeth cut through Wash's fishing line.

Reb yelled, "What *is* that thing?"

"Reb, get out of the water! He's coming for you!" Josh shouted.

The alligator, or whatever it was, had surfaced again. The bright round eyes seemed fastened on Reb this time. It charged toward him, mouth gaping open.

Reb let out a yell and splashed toward the bank. Then perhaps he stepped into a hole, for down he went.

At Josh's side, Sarah screamed, "Reb!" He glimpsed her fumbling for her bow, but she had left her weapon back with Meta and the babies and their equipment. So had everyone else—except for Josh himself.

Josh did not even think. His mind was not working fast enough. His hand was fast, however, and from its sheath he jerked the sword that he always carried. He leaped into the water and splashed past Reb. He lifted the sword over his head.

Now the creature was upon him. It had a purplish black mouth and throat that looked like a huge cavern armed with teeth. Josh brought down the sword with all of his might. He felt the jolt all the way to his shoulders, and the head of the beast disappeared under the surface. It came up at once, wounded but with teeth still snapping. Again and again Josh swung his blade. He was desperately aware that, if he missed, the creature's teeth would close on him.

But finally the animal sank, bubbling, and then Reb was at his side, shouting, "Get out of here, Josh! There are more of them!"

Josh looked up to see other pale alligators, or whatever they were, swimming toward them from the opposite bank.

The two boys splashed to shore. The others went running for their weapons, and the battle began. Some of the river monsters died from Sarah's arrows, and others from sword blades. Josh was aware that Gus was in the middle of the fray, slashing right and left and yelling at the top of his lungs.

When the last alligator retreated, Meta ran over to Gus as if he had been the only rescuer. "Oh, Gus, you saved us!"

Gus looked satisfied. "I guess I did, didn't I? Well, that's the way it is. Some of us are just born to be heroes."

Sarah snorted with disgust. She turned to Josh. She said, "You did wonderfully, Josh."

Reb came up and threw an arm over Josh's shoulder. "You saved my bacon that time," he said, beaming. Then he looked around at the dead beasts. "I wonder if they'd be good to eat."

"What an awful thought!" Sarah exclaimed.

"Well, they used to eat alligators down in Louisiana, I heard tell. These are just a kind of alligator."

"I just want to get away from here," Josh said. "Grab your fish, and let's go. Let's leave this river alone."

10
Surprise Attack

They found a shelter for the night. It was not exactly a cave but a hollow place in the side of a hill. At Josh's suggestion they built fires around the outside edge of their camp and placed the babies as close to the face of the hill as they could.

Sarah was trying to cook the fish that Gus and the boys had cleaned. She had discovered that her hands were still shaking. The monster alligators had been terrifying. "Look at my hands," she said, showing Meta, who was helping her.

Meta looked. "I know," she said sympathetically. "I know. I was so frightened just watching that I could hardly stand up. You were all so brave, though—especially Gus."

Casting a quick look at Meta, Sarah smiled. "Goél helped us. He always does. And, yes, Gus was very brave. You like Gus a great deal, don't you?"

"Oh yes, I do."

Sarah questioned the young woman while they worked. She found out that Meta had never had a sweetheart. Sarah thought Gus a rather unlikely candidate for this. But in spite of that, she had learned to appreciate the good qualities of the skinny young man. *He doesn't look like much,* she thought, *and he's awfully gloomy at times, but you can always count on him.*

"He's a fine young man, Meta," she said.

* * *

As everyone gathered around for the evening meal, Reb said again, "I wish I had some hush puppies."

"Maybe we can find some more grain and make some," Wash said.

"We haven't got time for that!" Dave snapped. "We've got to get out of here."

Josh was chewing on a piece of fish. It was actually delicious. The meat was white and not at all strong. "I wish I had some tartar sauce," he said. "That always was good with fish." Then he glanced over at Dave. "You know, Dave, sometimes the slowest way is the fastest way."

"I don't know what *that* means. I just know we need to get out of these woods."

"But we've got all these babies to take care of. If we try to go too fast, it'll be hard on them."

"We've got to make better time than we've been making. That's all there is to it, Josh. Surely you can see that."

Nothing Josh said seemed to make any impression on him.

Just before dark, Josh and Gus were milking the goats. Gus was stroking a nanny's head, while Josh milked steadily.

"You sure have turned into a good milker," Gus said. "Never any good at that myself."

"I thought you were good at everything, Gus."

"Well, I'm better at some things than other things."

"What do you figure you're best at?" Josh asked him. He expected some outlandish boast. He knew that Gus, along with always predicting disaster, held the opinion that he was quite a man.

82

But to his surprise, Gus said, "I suppose I'm best at writing poetry. That's why the fellows ran me out of the village."

"I thought it was because all the young ladies preferred you."

"That's part of the reason they preferred me," Gus said, stroking the rough coat of the goat. Then he shoved back his floppy hat, and his lean, cavernous features brightened with pleasure. He grinned broadly. "The girls liked me so much not just because I'm such a handsome fellow but because I wrote them nice little love poems."

"Let me hear one of them," Josh said.

Immediately Gus began to spout poetry:

"Your lips are prettier than palm leaves,
  And your eyes are like two pools of buttermilk.
  You have a neck like a swan,
  Legs like trees
  Teeth like mussel shells.
  Oh, how beautiful you are!"

It all sounded rather sappy to Josh, but he did not say so. "Well, I can see that the ladies would really like you, Gus. All those good looks and a poet too."

"That's true," Gus said sadly. "Sometimes I wish I wasn't so gifted." They continued milking, and after a while he commented, "It's a good thing we found another shelter. Dark's coming on, and I don't want to tangle with those bats. Those blasted alligators were bad enough."

Josh thought about the night dangers all the way back to camp. When they rejoined the others, he said, "I think we'd better have guards, Dave."

83

"Ah, nothing's going to happen," Dave said. "What could happen? Let's get a good night's sleep. We're all tired."

Sarah seemed to know that Josh had no intention of sleeping.

"I'll stay up, and we'll watch together," she said. "Then you can ask Reb or Wash to take a watch."

"That's a good idea."

When the others had rolled up in their blankets, Josh and Sarah stood watching. The stars were bright overhead. They glittered like diamonds.

Josh said, "There's the Big Dipper."

"It hasn't changed."

"Nope," Josh said. "Everything on earth has changed, but the stars are still up there."

"I've almost forgotten the constellations," Sarah said. "Do you remember any of them except the Big Dipper?"

"Well, there's Cassiopeia."

"Oh, yes! That's the one that looks just like a badly drawn W," Sarah said. "And there's Orion."

"Yep. Look at his belt. Those three stars in the middle."

"I always liked Orion."

For a long time they stood talking softly—first about the stars and then about life back in Oldworld. The time passed quickly, and before long, it seemed, Reb came to stand watch.

He held a sword. "You two go get some sleep," he said.

"Thanks, Reb. I *am* tired," Sarah said.

When she went off, Reb asked, "Josh, have you thought about it?"

"Thought about what?"

"About what we've talked about a dozen times. Dave's no good as a leader. He's strong, and he's the best swordsman I've ever seen, but he's just not a leader. You are."

"But I'm such a wimp. I can't shoot a bow like Sarah. I can't use a sword like Dave. I can't ride a horse like you can."

"That doesn't make no never mind," Reb said. "Some guys and some girls are just natural born leaders. They're not always the biggest or the strongest, but there's something in them that makes people want to follow them. I reckon that's what Goél saw in you, but you've let him down."

"You really think so, Reb?"

"Sure I think so. You think about it."

Josh did indeed think about it. He could not sleep for a long time. He lay with his hands locked beneath his head and stared up at the stars. Ever since the failure of the last mission, he knew he had allowed himself to be swamped with self-pity. It was one thing, however, to know it and something else to come out of it. *How does a guy stop feeling sorry for himself?* he wondered. He thought for a long time but came up with no answers.

The next day, as usual, they milked the goats, fed the babies, and started out on their journey. They traveled steadily all morning, stopping at intervals to rest. Josh saw no opportunity to exert leadership, and he spent most of the morning talking to Gus, who walked along beside him. He had come to like the skinny young man very much indeed.

Gus entertained him by quoting his love poems. He said, "I wrote a new one last night. It's for Meta."

"Can I hear it?"

85

"Of course you can't hear it. It's for her."

"But you let me hear your other poems."

"This is different. The first time a poem is said, it has to go to the one it's written for."

"Oh."

Josh watched as Gus dropped back then and fell into step with Meta. The young woman's face brightened. He could not hear what they were saying, but he knew that Gus was giving a rendition of *her* poem. He saw her face light up even more, and Josh thought, *Well, I'm glad somebody's happy on this trip.*

They fed the babies when they were hungry and stopped at noon to eat. It was the middle of the afternoon when Josh felt bold enough to move up beside Dave. "Remember, Dave, we've got to find shelter before nightfall."

"Know that. Plenty of daylight left."

Josh said firmly, "Dave, don't be bullheaded about this. We can't wait until dark to start looking."

Dave's face reddened. "Don't tell me what to do, Josh!"

"Well, somebody needs to!"

The two got into an argument. Josh knew everyone was listening, but no one jumped in to help settle it.

Finally Dave said, "Josh, I'm handling this, and I've already thought about it. Look ahead there. See that?"

Josh looked. He had been walking with Gus in the middle of the procession, and the trees were thick. Dave, at the front, had seen what Josh could not. It looked like a conical mountain.

Dave said with satisfaction, "*That's* where we're going to camp."

"Doesn't look like there're any trees on it," Josh muttered.

"But there'll be some *caves* in it. And it's not more than a mile away from here. So come on, Josh. Let's move."

Josh gave up and went back to walk with Sarah. He said, "Dave says we're going to camp at that little mountain up ahead. Says there will probably be caves in it."

"I'm glad he's thinking. We do need to stop early. We need time to care for the babies and feed them and get something cooked for ourselves. We have to gather firewood. It all takes a while."

"That was a beautiful poem, Gustavian," Meta said. "I never had a poem written to me before."

"Oh, I expect you'll have a lot of them." Then Gus said, "I like it when you use my whole name. I never cared much for Gus, but my full handle's too much for most people."

"Do you know any more poems?"

"Oh, sure." Gus began at once to spout verses.

The travelers left the thick forest and started across a field that was dotted with smaller trees. There was much wild grain growing there, and Josh made a note of that. "We'll come back and get grain and make mush again," he told Sarah.

There was no longer any need to walk single file, so Gus and Meta and the other Sleepers came up, and all formed a ragged line going across the field.

"That's sure a funny hill. The only one around here like it," Josh muttered. For some reason, an uncomfortable feeling came over him, and he said, "Dave, I think we'd better take this slow. Why don't we leave the babies and the girls here and go take a look at that hill?"

"Oh, don't be an old woman! It's just a hill."

Reluctantly Josh continued to walk toward the conical mound. Then, strangely, he noticed that the grass up ahead, now chest high, was moving. But there was no breeze. What was moving it?

Suddenly Gus let out a wild cry. "Look out!" he yelled. "Meta, get back! Everybody, get back! Take the babies back!"

"What is it, Gus?" Josh cried. He felt helpless holding Susie in his arms. Now was no time to fight.

"Here, let me take Susie," Sarah said quickly. "You go help Gus."

Josh deposited the baby in Sarah's free arm and then ran to join Gus, drawing his sword as he went. When he got closer to Gus's position, he saw Meta standing with horror in her eyes.

"What is it?"

"It's ants—giant ants!" she cried.

Josh yelled, "Get back! Take the babies back!" He then ran forward and almost dropped his sword at what he saw.

Gus was facing a monstrous ant. It was at least six feet tall, bright red, and was evidently a vicious insect. Gus demolished the creature with a single sweep of his sword, but others were coming through the tall grass, snapping their huge jaws as they came.

Now Josh understood. The great conical mound was an anthill. "Get the babies away!" he screamed again as he took his place beside Gus. Their swords flashed, and ants fell. But there were always more.

"We've got to hold them off, Gus—until they get the babies away."

Sarah, not Dave, quickly organized the retreat, and they rushed the infants back into the safety of the woods. "Meta," she said, "watch the babies." Then she cried to the rest, "Come, everybody! We've got to help Josh and Gus."

All the boys rushed back with her, their swords gleaming in the sun, to join Gus and Josh. For a while the battle was intense. The insects had skinny necks, and one good blow would decapitate them, but they kept coming. And coming. Sarah's arm grew tired from drawing her bow.

Josh stood firm in the line of battle. He had no time to think. It was just *slash slash slash* until finally the attack appeared to be over. The ants began to fall back.

But suddenly there was a cry behind him, and Josh whirled. The last ant had fastened its jaws on Dave's left forearm. Like a flash, Josh ran forward and brought his sword down on the ant's thin neck. The insect fell to the ground.

Dave stood staring at his torn arm. "He got me," he gasped.

"We've got to get that washed out, quick," Josh said. "In case there was some kind of poison in the bite."

By the time they were back to the shelter of the trees, Dave's face was pale as paper. He dropped to the ground, gasping, "It burns like fire!"

"Quick! Somebody bring a canteen of water," Gus said. "This kind of ant—the normal-sized ones—they do carry poison."

Dave lay with his eyes closed and his lips pressed tightly together as Abbey cleansed the ragged wound.

Josh tried to be comforting. "Don't worry, Dave. You'll be all right."

"I guess you'll have to be the leader now. I can't do a thing," Dave whispered.

Josh looked up, and his eyes met Sarah's. His jaw tightened. "Don't worry, Dave. It's all right. We'll take care of you. And Goél won't let us down."

11
The Unicorns

Dave has me worried," Josh said softly. He glanced down at the sleeping boy. "That arm's getting infected."

Sarah nodded. "I know. I wish we had a doctor. And how many times have we wished that since we've been in Nuworld? But maybe Gus and Meta can help. Both of them are pretty good with herbs."

"Is that where they've gone? To find some herbs?"

"Yes," she said. "They left about two hours ago."

"And I'll bet Gus had some cheerful remark to make about the whole situation."

"He said Dave will probably die if he doesn't find a certain plant. But I don't think he was just being his usual pessimistic self, Josh. I think he's really worried."

Dave was sleeping fitfully. His face was pale, and he was feverish. Abbey had cleansed the wound as well as she could, while wishing they had some miracle drug. But, of course, nothing like that was available in Nuworld.

"Where's Reb gone?"

"Out hunting," Sarah said. "I hope he gets something. I'm getting a little tired of goat's milk and mush. Though the babies don't seem to mind."

Josh said, "Let's take a walk. Then it'll be about time to change their diapers."

Sarah suddenly giggled. She quickly covered her mouth with a hand, but Josh had heard her.

"What are you laughing about? I don't see anything very funny in any of this."

"Oh, it's just that if they ever write the story of the Seven Sleepers, this won't sound very heroic."

"What won't?"

"I mean, here we are, the great Seven Sleepers that are celebrated in song all over Nuworld, and we're going to change diapers for eight babies."

Josh could not help smiling. "I'm just glad for the hot sun every day—it dries diapers fast."

Suddenly Sarah put her hand on Josh's arm. "You're more like your old self, Josh. It was wonderful the way you organized us after Dave got hurt . . . found us a place to hide . . . took care of Dave . . ."

Josh knew he was blushing, and he hated that. He always had. He said, "Wonder if I'll ever stop blushing. I feel like a fool."

"I hope you never do, Josh." Sarah smiled. "I think it's cute."

Josh opened his mouth, then shut it quickly and shrugged. "A leader's not supposed to be cute."

Sarah laughed. "I don't see why a leader can't be cute and brave at the same time."

For the first time since the defeat that had put him in such a state of discouragement, Josh suddenly felt warm and confident. "You know what?" he said quietly, his eyes fixed on her.

"What?"

"You do know how to cheer up a guy."

Sarah grinned. "Well, you can cheer me up when I get depressed. And both of us can cheer up Gus."

"Sometimes I think that's all an act he puts on. I don't think Gus is really gloomy at all. When you get right down to it, he's all talk. When I get down, he's able to cheer me up."

"He cheers up Meta too—with that awful poetry of his."

"Isn't it terrible?" Josh shook his head.

"She doesn't think so."

"I guess not."

They had reached the edge of the clearing now. Josh was keeping an eye out for any sort of awful monster when all of a sudden he heard a most unusual sound.

"What *is* that?" he asked.

"I don't know, but it sounds like . . . like a *horse* running."

Both stood there tensely, listening. The Sleepers had not seen any horses in this territory, but this sounded like nothing other than a horse running at full gallop.

Suddenly Reb Jackson burst from the trees on the other side of the clearing. But Reb was not alone. He was astride the most beautiful four-legged creature that Josh had ever seen.

"A unicorn!" Sarah cried out. "How beautiful it is!"

They stared at the approaching animal. It was snow white. It had a long white mane that flowed as it galloped toward them. But beautiful as the unicorn was, the most spectacular aspect about the creature was the long, twisted horn that grew from its forehead.

"Whoa up, boy!" Reb said. He slipped off the unicorn's back and clung to its silky mane. He patted the animal fondly, saying, "How about this for a mount?" His eyes were dancing.

"Reb, wherever did you find him?"

"Why, there's a whole herd of them about two miles farther along. Lots of open pasture down that way." He patted the unicorn again and said, "And you're a smart one too, aren't you, Flash?"

"Is that his name? Flash?" Sarah asked. She put out her hand. The horn looked terribly dangerous when the unicorn turned to her. But his lips drew back, and the beautiful animal nibbled at her hand.

"Oh, I wish I had an apple to give you! You're so beautiful."

"Flash is the name I call him, and he runs like one, too."

"How did you find him?"

Reb shrugged. "Just walked in on 'em." He stroked the unicorn's sleek side. "And when they all saw me, they didn't run like wild horses would. They walked right toward me. At first I was afraid they'd try to run me through with those horns. But they were just curious."

Flash reached over and nibbled at Reb's shoulder. Reb threw an arm around him and cried, "He's the best thing I've ever ridden. Better than an eagle. And he almost seems to know what I'm saying. I can't get over it!"

By this time, the other Sleepers came running and stood in a circle around the beautiful animal. Now everyone was there except Dave and Gus and Meta and the babies.

Reb answered their questions as quickly as he could. And, as he'd said, the unicorn with the bright brown eyes almost seemed to be listening and understanding what he was saying.

"They're sure the friendliest *wild* animals I've ever seen."

Abbey stroked Flash's nose. "He's so beautiful! How many more are there?"

"There must be twenty or thirty. This one seemed to be the leader."

"I'd sure like to see that herd," Josh said enviously.

"Come on, then. I'll take you. I know where they are."

"Someone will have to stay here and look after Dave and the babies," Josh said. "Let's take turns."

So the Sleepers went in shifts to visit the herd of unicorns. They were greeted by the animals enthusiastically. "Wild horses don't want anybody up on their backs," Reb said, "but these unicorns, they love it when you ride them. These critters are like dogs—they like people."

Sarah climbed onto the back of a beautiful palomino mare. "Come on, girl. Let's see what you can do." At the touch of her heels, the mare shot away. The gait was easy, but the unicorn took off in an explosion of speed. Sarah hung onto the mane and leaned forward like a jockey.

Josh mounted a black stallion and rode up beside her.

She grinned at him. "Oh, Josh, this is as much fun as riding eagles."

He yelled back, "They're the fastest thing on four legs I've ever seen. Even faster than a cheetah."

It was a wonderful day for the Sleepers. Everyone except Dave had a chance to ride. That night when they gathered back in the cave that Josh had found, they talked excitedly about the herd of unicorns.

"Of all the strange critters we've seen out here," Reb said, "these take the cake. They could win a race against any horse back in Oldworld. I never saw such speed."

Jake agreed, then said, "They're strong too. Wonder what they use that horn for? Defense?"

95

"Probably. They could do considerable damage with their horns if they took a notion. That thing's a foot and a half long and has a needle point on it."

"It's a good thing they're not mean," Abbey said. "They're so gentle and friendly."

"One thing's sure," Josh said. "They're not creatures that Dr. Korbo engineered. They're just sort of a mutant, maybe—like some of the other things we've seen."

"That's right," Sarah agreed quickly. "Nothing Dr. Korbo has made has been gentle like this. That wicked man has to be a servant of the Dark Lord."

They sat around talking for a while, and then Reb had an idea. "I'm wondering if we couldn't ride these unicorns out of here. It'd sure beat walking."

Josh gnawed on his lip. "I don't know, Reb. It's one thing just to ride around in that valley they live in, but taking them away from their home might somehow upset the balance of nature."

"The valley *is* their home," Jake said. "But it's something to think about anyway."

They did think about it for a time, but not long. Everyone was exhausted from their busy day.

"One thing for sure, that mare's milk is a welcome relief from goat's milk," Reb said. "And the unicorns don't seem to mind sharing it with us."

They had discovered that many of the mares had foals. The foals were cute, looking like their parents except for just a small knot between their eyes where the horn would be later. The mares would stand patiently while they were milked, and their milk was absolutely delicious.

"Not near as strong tasting as that goat's milk," Reb said. "I bet Sammy will like it." Sammy was Reb's particular charge, and, like the others, he thought "his" baby was the strongest and best looking of all the infants.

"I think we'll stay here and rest up at least one more day," Josh said. "Dave's not able to travel anyhow." He got up, saying, "I think I'll go check on him."

Dave didn't improve during the night. But the next morning he drank some of the fresh unicorn's milk, and that seemed to make his eyes brighter. "My arm's so sore I can hardly move it," he said.

"Take it easy, Dave. Gus and Meta found some herbs. They're fixing them right now. Gus says they'll speed up the healing," Josh told him. Then he went to watch Meta and Gus shred leaves from various plants.

"I didn't think anyone knew as much about plants as I do," Gus said. "But you do."

"My grandmother—Viona—she taught me a lot about them."

"You'd be handy to have around. Somebody's always getting sick. When I get sick, which I probably will pretty soon—I'm not feeling too well, you know—you can take care of me."

Meta smiled. "Let's go see our patient," she said. "I think this will help him."

Josh followed them inside, where Meta made a compress out of one kind of leaf and bound it over Dave's wound. With another kind they made a brew of strong tea. The aroma of it filled the air as it bubbled over the fire.

"Here," Gus said. "If you drink enough of this, you'll be fine. It'll make you good looking. That's the secret of my good looks, you know."

Dave did not seem impressed by this, but he managed to grin. "I'll look forward to that, Gus," he said.

The compress and frequent drinks of the strong tea did seem to do wonders for Dave. By the next morning he was able to sit up and felt like walking around a bit. "My arm's stiff," he said, "but I feel much better."

"That's good," Josh said. "We were all worried about you."

Dave looked rather embarrassed. "I've been kind of a pain in the neck lately, Josh. I'm sorry. I just got carried away, I guess."

"That's all right, Dave," Josh said quickly. "We all get carried away at times."

Sarah and Abbey and Meta were at a small creek washing diapers when Sarah looked up to see the beautiful palomino that she had named Lady trotting toward them. With delight Sarah jumped up and ran to meet the unicorn. "Lady," she said and stroked her nose, "you came for a visit. All by yourself."

The girls admired the mare for a while, then went back to work. Lady watched curiously. From time to time she would come close, sniff at one of them, and then stamp her hoof.

"She seems so curious. They love us," Sarah said.

"I think they love everybody," Meta said. "They've got love in their eyes."

The girls had just finished their washing, when there was a sharp animal cry. Then a huge weasel with a long body, sharp teeth, and reddish eyes emerged from the bushes and came straight for them.

Meta screamed. Abbey screamed. Sarah made a frantic grab for her sword, then remembered she had left it back in the cave. *We have no weapons!* she thought wildly.

Lady reacted, too. She lowered her head and charged the vicious looking animal. The eighty- or ninety-pound weasel was fearless. He sprang to meet the unicorn.

Lady's needle-sharp horn struck the weasel in the breast. It fell and lay still. The unicorn backed away, her eyes fiery. The girls had not needed weapons.

They ran to the unicorn and began petting her.

"Oh, thank you, Lady," Sarah cried. "You saved our lives."

Later on, when the boys came to view the body of the weasel, Reb looked at Lady and grinned. Her eyes were bright, and she seemed to have suffered no ill effects from the encounter. He stroked her mane. "Well, you're mighty pretty, Lady, but I guess you can do just about anything when you take a notion."

Lady stamped her hooves and nibbled at Reb's hat. She plucked it off his head.

"Hey, take it easy!" he said. "That's my favorite hat."

The unicorn dropped it and then began to pull at his hair.

Sarah laughed at the sight. "She loves you, Reb."

"She's a handy critter to have around," Reb said. "I'd like to turn her loose on some of those squirrels."

"She could handle them," Sarah said proudly. "I think a unicorn can do most anything."

12
Josh's Plan

S arah looked over to where Josh was changing Susie's diaper again. "You don't mind doing that, do you?"

He looked up with surprise. "Nope." Then he grinned.

"Most boys would think that's sissy."

"Most boys can think what they want to."

"That's what I've always liked about you, Josh," Sarah said.

"What? That I can change diapers?"

"No. That you're not afraid to do things that other people might not understand."

Josh finished his job and joggled Susie on his knee. She gurgled, and he leaned forward, looking into her mouth. "I wonder when you're going to start cutting teeth. That won't be any fun." Then he looked back at Sarah. "You're not altogether right about what you said. I used to be terribly worried about what people thought about me. You, for instance."

"Me! Why me?"

"When you first came to our house, back before we came to Nuworld. Do you remember?"

"I remember I was awfully afraid. My parents were off in Africa, and I was coming to live with a strange family. I didn't know any of you, and I thought you might be—well, I didn't know what you'd be."

"I didn't know you felt like that at the time," Josh said. "The first time I saw you, I got all choked up. I always was afraid of pretty girls, and you were the prettiest girl I'd ever seen."

Sarah laughed at that. "You must not have seen many pretty girls."

"Anyway," Josh said. "I don't know why, but I thought I had to be tough."

"I remember that too. You swaggered around and tried to talk tough, but I knew you weren't." Sarah stood up. "Let's put these babies down on the floor with the others."

For a while they watched the eight babies try to crawl around. Josh said, "It would have been terrible if that magician Korbo had done something to one of these kids."

"I know. He must be a monster himself. But that's what the Dark Lord does to people."

About that time Gus walked into the cave. He was carrying fresh milk. "That's funny."

"What's funny, Gus?"

"Those mares. The way they came over here all by themselves just now—practically asking to be milked. I appreciate the goats, but this is sure better." He held up the jug and said, "When we leave here, I'm going to miss unicorn milk. Of course, probably the herd will up and leave *us* anytime now. Might as well expect that."

Josh didn't answer, and Gus sat down beside him. "And you know we've got to leave here sooner or later, don't you, Josh?"

"I know. And it's worrying me a lot. I just can't make up my mind . . ."

Gus did not say anything else. He got up shortly and went to find Meta.

Meta was cutting up leaves for salad when Gus found her.

"I've written you another poem, Meta."

"Oh, let's hear it! I love your poetry."

Gus had not written down the poem, but it was firmly in his mind. He quoted the verse and winked at her. "How about that?"

"That's the most beautiful poem I ever heard."

"You said that about the last poem I wrote for you."

"Well, every poem that you write is better than the next one."

"Wait a minute! *That's* not right."

"Oh, no! That would mean your poetry was getting worse." Meta laughed and put her hand over her mouth. "I mean every one is better than the *last* one."

"Well, now, that's more like it." Gus sat down beside Meta and watched her finish her work. He took off his hat and put it down by his feet. His lank hair lay over his shoulders.

"You need your hair cut," she told him.

"What for?"

"Because it would make you look better."

Gus stared at her. "I thought I looked good enough already."

"Oh, you do," Meta said, "but I think if I could trim your hair neatly, it would improve even you."

"It would?"

"Oh yes. I think so."

"Well, have at it."

Meta ran to fetch some scissors, and soon she had given Gus a very respectable haircut. She brushed his hair back and said, "Now, that looks much better."

"I guess I'll have to write a poem. I'm going to call it *Ode to a Haircut*."

"Will I be in it?" Meta smiled shyly.

"You'll be the star of it. You know, we make a great team. Me to write the poetry, and you to listen to it."

"Yes, we do, Gus. I've never told you this, but I was so sad after my grandmother died. But then you came along, and every day you've cheered me up. You'll never know how much it's meant to me."

"I'll write a poem about it. I'll call it *Poem*."

"Just *Poem?*"

"That's right. Just *Poem*. It'll go like this . . ."

Meta sat listening, her eyes warm, as what passed for poetry in Gus's mind rolled from his mouth. It was not very good poetry, but she did not care. It was hers.

They rested for two more days to be sure Dave was well enough to travel.

Josh was standing looking off into the distance when he came by.

"You needn't hold up traveling for me anymore," Dave announced. "I can move this arm as good as before. It wasn't my sword arm anyway, Josh."

"That's good. You had us all worried. Those ants are mean critters. We'll be sure to detour around that anthill when we go."

"I sure was wrong about that one." Dave rubbed his chin thoughtfully and said, "I've finally come to understand why Goél picked you to be the leader."

Josh was startled. "Why?"

"Because you *are* the leader. It's that simple." Dave shrugged his broad shoulders. "Some just have it, and some don't, and you've got it."

"I don't know about that . . ." Josh muttered.

"In any case, I got all the craziness out of my system. Now whatever you say is what we'll do."

"That's nice of you to say that, Dave. But I'll always be glad for any suggestions. I wish I had an easy answer to our problems."

"There aren't many easy answers to big problems, are there?"

"No. Not many."

All day Josh just walked around by himself. Everyone seemed to know he was thinking and planning, and no one wanted to disturb the process.

At supper time, he came back and joined the group seated around the fire. Reb had brought down a wild pig that afternoon, so they enjoyed a good meal.

The others talked about the babies, or about the unicorns, or about past adventures. Josh said little. He was still thinking hard.

Finally Josh cleared his throat, and everyone looked at him. He found he had difficulty speaking, but he finally began. "I've got something to tell you. It's something . . . well, something new. And it's going to be hard."

The Sleepers looked at each other, and Sarah said, "What is it, Josh? You can tell us."

"Well, I've been thinking about these babies. There are more children, aren't there, Meta?"

"Oh, yes. The villagers are scattered everywhere, trying to hide them. The people are all terrified of Dr. Korbo."

"They're afraid he'll come and take their children."

Meta nodded silently, and a murmur ran through the group.

After a moment Reb muttered, "I never thought of it that way. We're saving eight of them, but all he has to do is go out and get some more."

"That's right," Josh said quickly. He took a deep breath and said, "We've got to keep him from doing that."

Sarah looked amazed. "How could we do that, Josh?"

"Miss Viona said we were the Sent Ones. I think she knew something even then, and I think Goél is in all of this—even though he hasn't come around to give us any direct orders." He said tightly, "I don't think it's an accident that we came to this place. Even though Goél never specifically told us to come."

"Maybe you're right," Jake spoke up. "If we hadn't gotten defeated on our last mission, we never would have come here. Maybe that's what Goél had in mind all along. Maybe good will come out of that defeat yet."

"That's right, Josh," Dave said warmly. "And you're back as leader again. I want to speak for myself and say I'm willing to do whatever you think is right. You're the leader."

Josh flushed. "That's real nice of you to say that, Dave. I can't say that I've heard from Goél. He seems to be withholding himself right now."

"I think he wants us to grow up," Sarah said quietly. Then she asked, "What are you thinking, Josh?"

"We've got to go back," he said, "and beard the lion in his den."

"What does *that* mean?" Meta asked. Without waiting for an explanation, she said, "We can't go back! We'll be caught! Dr. Korbo will take the babies. We're almost out of his land now. It isn't too far to the border."

"I don't think we're meant to leave yet. I don't think Goél would want *any* babies hurt by that crazy man. What we've got to do—" Josh took a deep breath and looked around "—is to arrest him."

"Arrest him!" Reb's voice rose above the others. "You mean like we were sheriffs and he was an outlaw?"

"Exactly that!"

"But he's well guarded," Meta cried. "He lives in a castle, and there are awful monsters guarding it. And his men—he doesn't have many, but they're evil."

"We can't let that stop us," Josh said. "It all came to me when I was holding Susie earlier today. She's so pretty and sweet, and I thought about what that magician might have done to her. It made me very angry. And then I thought, *Well, there are lots of other babies out there. He could hurt them, too.*"

"I believe you've hit it, Josh," Sarah said. "Before we go, we've got to do something to save all the babies."

"Are you all with me, then?" he asked. "It's going to be dangerous, and we may not all make it. But this looks like something we've got to do."

A murmur of agreement went around the circle.

Suddenly Gus clapped his hands. "This calls for a poem," he said. "It'll be called *The Saga of Gus*, and it'll be about how he stood up to the evil magician in his castle."

"Just a minute. Before you start this ode," Reb said, "are you intending to do this all by yourself, Gus?"

"Oh, no," Gus said. "You can all come along. We'll probably all get killed, but it'll make a good poem. I'd better write it before we go."

That brought a laugh from everybody.

"You write the poem, and you be the hero of it, Gus," Josh told him. "If you hadn't taken us in, I don't know if we would have gotten this far."

"Well, it all goes to show that there's more to me than just a pretty face." Gus nodded contentedly and then began composing his poem.

13

The Village

The babies had all been fed and were sleeping quietly. The Sleepers, joined by Gus and Meta, sat around in a circle. Over the fire some deer stew bubbled quietly in a pot. Its delicious aroma drifted into the cave, and from time to time Reb went out and stirred it. "Just about right," he said. "Nothing like venison stew—unless it's possum stew."

Josh had been quiet and thoughtful. Looking around, he thought he saw doubt on the faces of several. "I know that this is going to be a tough mission," he said, "but we all agreed we've got to do it."

"The thing that bothers me," Jake said, "is how we're going to fight and take care of our nursery at the same time."

"I know," Josh said. "That bothers me too, and so far I haven't come up with any answer for it."

"I know what we *might* do," Meta said. She rarely spoke up when others were talking, and everyone looked somewhat surprised.

"If you've got any ideas, Meta, let's have them," Josh encouraged her. "You know this country better than anyone else."

"There's a small village on the outskirts of the magician's kingdom. He knows it's there, but he doesn't send his men to it as often as he does most—because it's so far from the castle."

"And are you thinking we might get these villagers to help with the babies?" Sarah asked quickly.

"They would be glad to do it, I think," Meta said slowly. "They are terrified of Dr. Korbo—as everyone is—and they're good people."

"What about the men in the village?" Josh said. "Do you think they would help us fight?"

"They might try. Some of them hunt with bows, so they could be of some help. But many are old, and some are too young."

"Any help we could get would be appreciated."

Then Sarah said, "Meta, who knows the inside of the castle better than anyone else?"

"As a matter of fact, there's an old man who lives in that very village I spoke of. He was a servant in the castle for many years. Dr. Korbo used him very badly, I'm afraid. And then when he got old and sick, he threw him out. The village took him in."

"I'd like to talk to that man," Josh said. "We need to know what's inside the castle. Assuming we could get in, we'll be lost if we don't know which way to go."

"That's a good idea," Dave said eagerly. "We could draw the castle plan on paper at his direction and memorize it."

"Is everyone agreed then that we go to this village?"

"It is a very long way," Meta warned. "It would take a long time with the babies."

Josh said, "Well, one idea Reb had earlier might help with distance." He turned to Reb. "Do you think the unicorns would carry us there?"

Reb looked surprised, but he said, "Why not? They like us. They're not afraid of riders. And they seem to love human company."

"I think that's a wonderful idea, Josh!" Sarah said. Excitement brought color to her cheeks. "It would be an easy journey on the unicorns."

110

"All right, then," Josh said firmly. "If the unicorns seem comfortable leaving their valley, we'll do it."

"When do we leave?" Wash asked. "I'd like to get this thing over with."

"I don't know how long the trip will take, but I don't see why we couldn't leave in the morning," Josh said. "Another good thing—if the unicorns will take us, we'll have fresh mare's milk."

"The mares would have to bring their foals along," Reb said. "You know, I think the whole herd might go. Flash is sort of the head unicorn. Wherever he goes, the rest will probably follow."

"That would be great." Now Josh grew excited himself. "Let's make some plans!" He stood and began to pace back and forth. "Now, the goats . . . the goats can't keep up with the unicorns . . . we can just turn them loose in the grassy valley where they can fend for themselves . . ."

Early the next morning, the Seven Sleepers, Meta, and Gus bundled up the babies and led the goats and walked to the valley of the unicorns. Flash and Lady and then the entire herd moved toward them at once.

"Hey, Flash, old buddy. Would you like to go for a nice little trip?" Reb asked.

Flash blew through his lips, making a blubbering sound, and Reb turned and grinned. "He says it's OK with him."

It took some time to get everybody mounted. A rider would have to get on, and then someone else would hand up one of the infants.

"Real nice how easy all this is with these unicorns," Reb said. "If you tried to do this with wild horses, they'd break your neck."

"Just another sign that we're doing the right thing," Josh said.

Only Gus was a little apprehensive. "I don't know about all this," he said. He stood looking at the mottled brown unicorn that had evidently taken a liking to him. "I never was on a horse but once. And he up and threw me off and broke my leg."

"Oh, come, Gus," Meta said, smiling. "Get on. You can write a poem about it."

Gus's face brightened. "That's right. I could." He awkwardly struggled onto the back of the brown unicorn and began to mumble the lines of his poem.

It was as Reb had said. The entire herd of about twenty full-grown stallions and mares along with their foals did follow their unicorn leader. Reb, mounted on Flash, rode in front, and they set out at a comfortable pace.

"The unicorns make a pretty parade," Josh said to Sarah, who was riding alongside him. Some of the unicorns were glistening white, others jet black, and others palomino. Others were colored still differently. Mares and stallions alike had the long silver horn that gave them such an unusual appearance.

"They are so beautiful and so *good*."

"I hate to think what Dr. Korbo would make out of them if he had the chance. Something monstrous, I'm sure."

"But we're going to stop him, aren't we, Josh?"

"You're right," he said. "Korbo's day is over. He just doesn't know it yet."

They made very good time that first day. It would have taken a week for them to go as far as they did had they been walking.

It was late afternoon of the next day when at last

Meta said, "The village is there. Ahead. You can see the houses."

It was a small village, having no more than twenty huts, and the few villagers came out with fear in their eyes. They were small for the most part and dressed poorly. Although some of the men held staves and had bows, they were obviously not a fighting crew. Josh could see that they were awed by the sight of the unicorns.

Meta called out, "It's me—Meta! How are you, Chief Canto?"

The man she had spoken to was a little larger than the other men and held a sword in his hand. "Why, Meta," he said, "where is your grandmother?"

Sadly, Meta told him. She slipped off the unicorn, holding her baby in her arm.

"They look very dangerous, these . . . horses," Canto said. "Their horns could kill a man."

"They're very gentle," Meta assured him. She turned to the others and said, "This is Josh. He is the leader of this group." She went around and introduced each one, then said, "Josh, perhaps you'd better explain . . . about us and the babies . . ."

Josh said, "Chief Canto, we have come to help you if we can."

"Indeed, we need help," Canto said. He seemed weary. "Our people are in poor condition here."

"Is it the magician, Korbo?"

"Yes. He takes what he wants and leaves us to starve. And now he is threatening to take our children."

"That's what we have come to stop," Josh announced firmly.

Canto's eyes flew open. "I fear that you cannot stop the magician!"

"I believe we can—with your help. Meta tells me that you have an older man here who knows the inside of the castle well."

"Yes. His name is Benti. He is very old indeed."

"We would like to talk with him."

Canto had no objections, and soon Josh and the other Sleepers were surrounding an old man who had been sitting in the sun outside a rude hut. He had white hair, and his face was creased with many lines.

"Yes. I lived in Dr. Korbo's castle for many years. I know every inch of it."

"Can you describe it to us?" Dave brought out a sheet of paper and a pencil. He listened and drew lines as Benti described the interior of the castle.

When the elderly man had told all that he knew, both Josh and Dave said, "Thank you, Benti."

"You are the enemies of the magician?"

"We feel he is bad for all people—even for the beasts."

"Indeed he is." Pain came into Benti's eyes as he looked around the village. "These are good people here, but they have had little chance."

"They will have a chance now," Josh said with more confidence than he felt.

When the Sleepers went back, Josh found Meta talking with Chief Canto. "The chief says that he will have the women here care for the babies while we arrest Dr. Korbo," she said.

"That would be a great favor indeed, Chief." Josh hesitated, then said, "Would it also be possible for some of your warriors to come and help us take the castle?"

Chief Canto seemed embarrassed. "They are very much afraid of the magician. They know that he can do terrible things to them."

"That is why he needs to be removed from power," Josh said.

"We will talk about it. I myself will go with you, but we must convince the rest of the village."

The convincing took a great deal of time.

"The men are terrified of Korbo," Sarah said to Josh. "I'm not sure how much help they'll be."

"I'm not, either. But any help will be appreciated."

Josh and Sarah wandered around the village, visiting the babies, who had been placed with different families. They stopped by to chat again with the old man, Benti.

"Tell us more about the castle, Benti, if you can. Anything will be a help. How it is guarded, for example."

"It was never a good place, but it has been worse with this magician."

"Our problem is that we've got to get inside, and we don't know exactly how many guards there are."

Benti had lost most of his teeth, but he said vigorously, "As you surely know, the guards are not the greatest problem. There are very few guards in the courtyard guarding the castle."

"Why is that?" Sarah asked. "You would think Dr. Korbo would have many guards."

"He does not need guards there. No one can get through the courtyard because of the lion-headed bulls."

"Lion-headed bulls! You never mentioned those."

"You do not know about them?" Benti seemed surprised. "I thought everyone knew about the lion-headed bulls."

An image jumped into Josh's mind, but he could not see it clearly. "Let me get this straight. These are bulls with heads like lions, teeth and all?"

"They have the huge teeth of lions and the sharp horns of bulls. They are very fierce. They are very frightening. No one can stand against them."

"I see what you mean, Benti. Dr. Korbo really wouldn't need a great number of human guards, then."

"He has some, but the magician doesn't like people. He despises the guards he has. He despises everyone."

"So if we could get past these lion-headed bulls, then it could be fairly easy to get to the magician himself."

"Why would you want to get to him?" Benti said. "He will turn you all into something horrible."

"We must take a chance on that."

"Well, his living quarters are at the very top of the castle."

"Have you ever been inside his rooms?"

"Where he lives? Yes. Many times, cleaning. He has strange things up there. I don't know what they are, but there are many glass containers. It is where he takes the animals."

"That must be where he does his genetic engineering, making beasts out of good animals," Josh said thoughtfully.

"I'm an old man and will not live long. You are a young man, but you will not live long, either. Not if you go into that castle."

But Josh suddenly felt a new burst of confidence. "It will be all right. Goél will be with us," he said.

"Who is Goél?"

"Our great guide and helper. He is the one who is going to enable us to overcome the wizard."

"I hope it is so. Dr. Korbo is an evil magician and has caused much grief."

"Well, his days are over," Josh said, getting up.

As Josh and Sarah walked back toward the meeting with the chief, he said, "I've got a good feeling about this, Sarah."

Sarah smiled. "I do, too. We haven't come this far to be beaten by a second-rate magician!"

14

The Battle for the Castle

The war party lay hidden in the darkness.

Both the Sleepers and the villagers who had agreed to come and fight had ridden the unicorns. The men had been frightened of the animals at first but had quickly learned to trust them.

Josh wanted to attack at dawn. He'd explained his plan of attack to his ragtag army the night before, and most had appeared rather doubtful. The villagers listened, but he was not sure how much they understood.

Now, as the first signs of light began to show in the east, he called together the Sleepers along with Gus. "I want to go over this one more time," he said. "We only have a few minutes."

They all drew closer, and Josh felt a sudden wave of affection for these friends with whom he had shared such dangers. He wanted to make a speech about how much he liked them and trusted them, but somehow he could not say that.

Instead, he said, "Here's what we'll do. Reb, you see the walls. It's just as Benti said."

Reb peered into the growing light. The wall that surrounded the castle was fifteen feet high. Along the top of the wall, sharp spikes were set every few feet.

"Can you throw a rope over one of those spikes, do you think, Reb?"

"Why do you ask me a thing like that? You know I can. It's what comes afterward that I don't like."

"That's not your worry. You put the rope over, and then it's my turn."

"Josh, are you sure you can climb that rope?" Dave asked. "I've done a little climbing, and it's hard to pull yourself up hand over hand."

"I can do it," Josh said, trying to sound confident. He was determined to do the most dangerous part himself.

"But why don't we all climb over the wall?"

"No. All I've got to do is open those gates. That's the heart of the plan. If we all try to go up, they're sure to hear us, and the guards will be drawn out of the castle."

"It doesn't sound like they need any guards," Wash said gloomily. "Not with those lion-headed bulls that Benti was talking about. They sound like mean creatures."

"I don't plan to let them get at me. They're probably just wandering around in there like cattle. And if I'm quiet, I can drop down in front of the gate without their seeing me. I'll open it, and that's where the rest of you come in."

"It sounds kind of shaky to me," Jake said. "Too many things can go wrong."

"Jake, this is our best shot. It's the unicorns that will make it work."

The idea had come to Josh after much thought. From what he had heard from Benti about the enormous bulls with their sharp teeth and pointed horns and bad tempers, he could not figure a way to get past them. And then he had thought of the unicorns.

He remembered that the unicorn Lady had polished off the giant weasel with absolutely no problem at all. And he said to himself, *With that terrible horn on their heads, they could whip anything.*

120

He had gone over the plan before, but now he repeated it. "We saw how that unicorn defended you, Sarah, and I'm trusting that they'll all jump right at those lion-headed bulls in the same way."

"But what if they don't?" she asked.

"We'll just have to believe that they will. We don't have any other chance."

"I'm afraid for you, Josh," Sarah said quietly. "Inside that wall."

"We all are," Abbey echoed. "You're taking the worst chance of all."

"That's why I'm the leader," Josh said. "I found that out at last."

"I wish you wouldn't do it," Reb said. "Let *me* climb the rope."

"Let *me*," Dave offered.

"No. You'll be mounted on the lead unicorn, Reb. You've got to lead the charge. Flash trusts you. As soon as that gate's open, you've got to be through it, and the rest will follow. At least that's what I'm hoping for."

The light was getting more evident now, and Josh took a deep breath. "Here we go. Gus, you got anything cheerful to share?"

For once in his life, Gustavian Devolutarian had nothing depressing to say. He came up and put an arm around Josh. "Except for me, you're the best looking fellow around here, and I think you're a great leader. It's going to work fine, Josh. We're going to arrest that magician, and everything's going to be great."

"Will wonders never cease!" Josh breathed. "You know how to make a fellow feel good."

The light was growing every moment, and Josh knew there was no time to lose. "Come on then, Reb. Do your stuff."

Josh and Reb emerged from the woods, Reb carrying his lariat. Nothing was stirring, not even a dog, and they reached the base of the wall without raising any alarm.

"Drop your loop over that spike," Josh whispered.

Reb measured the distance and started swinging the rope. He released it, and it flew upward. It dropped exactly over one of the spikes, and he drew it down tight. "There you go, buddy," he said. He put a hand on Josh's shoulder and said, "You're a good egg."

"You too, Reb. Now, get back to Flash, and when that gate opens, you bring them in."

Josh did not wait to watch Reb run back for the cover of the trees. He grasped the rawhide rope in one hand and placed one foot on the rock wall. Drawing himself up, he mounted as quietly as he could. His arms began to grow tired when he was three-fourths of the way up, so he stopped and rested a few seconds. By the time he got to the top and was able to reach one of the spikes and pull himself up, he was out of breath. He looked down the line of spikes, and then he sat on the edge of the wall. The castle loomed before him. He looked upward and saw where the magician's quarters were located at the top.

Then he looked down, and his breath almost left him. Milling around below in the castle courtyard were some of the strangest creatures that he could imagine. They were indeed like huge bulls, but their heads were not the heads of cattle. They were lionlike, though they had sweeping horns like a Texas longhorn. Any one of them could tear with his teeth or slash with his horns or trample him with his giant hoofs. The guard animals seemed not to have heard him, and he was grateful for that.

A wave of fear came over Josh then. But he over-
came it, as he had often done before, by remembering
who would help him. He pulled up the lariat and muttered under his breath, "Well, Goél, here we go."

Josh moved to his left, crawling on his hands and
knees and wriggling around the spikes. Sharp stones
were also embedded in the top of the wall, so that soon
he'd scraped his hands. The knees of his pants were
cut to ribbons. He clamped his lips together and
crawled on. At last he reached the gate. He looked
toward the trees and could see movement there. He
knew the timing would have to be right, so he waved,
gesturing with his arm for Reb's company to come forward. At once he saw a flash of white, and there came
Reb, riding the lead unicorn. Others were following.

Josh looked down and back. Several of the beasts
were still moving about uneasily. He did not know
whether they heard the sound of the approaching
hooves or not, but there was no time for delay. He
looped the lasso over a spike and stepped out into
space above the castle courtyard. He slid down the
rope, which burned his cut and bleeding hands.

Josh's feet hit the stone courtyard, and he spun
around. One of the lion-headed beasts had spotted him,
he saw. It tossed its horns and started his way. Already
he could hear its angry snorts.

Next, Josh whirled toward the gates. A huge bar
held the doors in place, and he threw all his strength
into lifting it. He flung the freed bar to the ground and
pushed the gates open.

As the doors swung wide, the snorting beast, now
charging full speed toward him, let out a mighty roar.
Josh pressed his back against the wall, knowing he was
helpless.

And then a white unicorn with Reb Jackson on his back burst through the open gate. Reb was waving his hat. And then the bull and the unicorn met with a mighty clash.

For a moment Flash was pushed backward by the sheer weight of the awful looking animal. But the horn of the unicorn had done its work, and the lion-headed bull fell over.

Josh pressed himself against the wall as the whole unicorn herd thundered in. He saw Jake, on the back of a coal black unicorn, yell and scream as his animal engaged in battle. He saw Dave . . . Wash . . . then Sarah on Lady . . . Abbey . . .

Now the courtyard was filled with the bellowing of the bulls. They were indeed ferocious creatures, and many of the unicorns were slashed by the horns. Others were bitten by the lion-bulls' sharp teeth. But the unicorns were very fast and very brave. They also seemed able to read each other's minds. When one unicorn was suffering a defeat, another would come in from the side and attack with his horn.

And then Josh realized that he could not wait for the battle to be over. He drew his sword and ran across the courtyard toward the door of the castle.

"I've got to get to the magician," he muttered. "He's heard all this, and he'll be waiting for us."

15

The Magician

As soon as Josh reached the castle doorway, he sprang inside and saw a set of stairs running upward.

"Josh, wait for me!"

Josh looked back to see Sarah. Her face was pale. Across her shoulder was her bow.

"Sarah, what are you doing in here?"

"The battle is almost over out there, but it's not over in here."

Even as she spoke, three burly men appeared, waving swords.

Sarah was helpless. She couldn't use her bow in such tight quarters.

Josh managed to fend them off but was backing up when he heard a shrill scream from the doorway. *That's Reb,* he thought without looking. *That's Reb, giving his rebel yell. Thank you, Goél.*

Reb threw himself into the fray, and he and Josh together managed to put the guards out of action. Then the boys and Sarah ran for the stairs.

"It's a long way up to the top of this thing," Reb panted.

The stairs were long, and on every landing they had to fight off a guard. Dealing with the few human guards inside the castle turned out to be almost as bitter a fight as the battle outside with the lion-headed bulls.

At some time, Josh became aware that the rest of the Sleepers had joined them. Gus too was in the thick of things. He did not carry a sword but a small ax that had a blade on one side and a sharp point on the other. But soon he had received a wound along his arm.

"Oh, you're hurt," Abbey cried.

Gus frowned at the wound. "Probably a little poison in there, too, I expect—but that'll just be more of a challenge, don't you think?"

Finally the Sleepers fought their way to what Josh thought must be the last landing. Here was a large open area, and beyond that was a huge door, which he was relatively sure led to the magician's laboratory. And here, it appeared, Korbo had placed most of his guards.

"We've got to get to that door!" he shouted. "All right, Sleepers, let's have at it."

Arrows hissed, and swords clashed. Some of the villagers arrived then and valiantly threw themselves into the fighting. The guards refused to give up.

The battle continued to rage until finally the weight of the invaders began to tell. One of the servants of the magician threw down his sword and cried out, "Don't kill me! I give up!"

As if at a sign, the rest of the guards did the same.

Josh yelled, "Don't kill them! Make them prisoners."

Soon the villagers had rounded up the surrendered men and bound their hands.

"Take them downstairs. We'll be there soon," Josh commanded.

"Now for the magician," Sarah said. "Wherever he might be."

"Right," Josh said grimly. He crossed to the huge door, lifted his foot, and then kicked it open. He entered, followed by the Sleepers and Gus, to see Dr. Korbo, the magician, drawn up before another large door that opened onto a balcony.

Korbo was a tall, lean man dressed completely in

black. He wore a sharp-pointed hat, and hatred flashed from his eyes.

"You'll pay for this!" he cried.

"No. *You're* going to pay for what you've done, Korbo," Josh said.

"Who are you? What are you doing in my castle?"

"We are the servants of Goél, and we have come to liberate the people and the poor beasts that you've enslaved."

"Goél! I know of no Goél!"

"You will know him soon, because you are going to meet him."

"What do you mean by that?" Korbo snarled.

"I mean we're taking you to him, and your fate will rest in his hands."

The magician drew himself up. "I will never surrender to this Goél or to anyone else! I am a servant of the Dark Lord."

Sarah asked quietly, "Why did you do such terrible things to the animals of your country?"

"You would not understand. I am a scientist, and we scientists do not live by the rules of other people."

"You're not a scientist. Scientists like to help people," Jake said. "You're just full of meanness and hate."

Korbo glared at them all. "Get out of my castle!"

"I'm afraid not, Korbo. We're taking you with us to Goél. He can take that evil out of you. If you are willing, you could become a better man."

The magician laughed wildly. It was obvious that he was not normal. "I will never go with you!" he said.

"Reb, you and Dave bring him along."

Reb and Dave advanced on the magician, but Korbo backed out onto the balcony. He continued to back up until he had reached the railing. "Stay away from me!" he screamed. "I won't go with you!"

"Look, Korbo," Josh said. "Goél can help you. You don't have to stay the way you are."

"I want to stay the way I am."

"So you can experiment on helpless babies?" Josh asked. "Don't you see how wrong that is?"

"I am a magician and a scientist. I obey only the Dark Lord."

"Just bring him, guys." Josh sighed. "There's no reasoning with him."

But Dave and Reb never had a chance to get to Korbo. Without warning, a monster bat swooped down from the sky. Evidently it had been searching for prey, and now it dove toward Korbo.

"Look out, Korbo! It's a bat!" Josh shouted.

The magician looked up, but he had no time to do anything else. The bat seized him by the throat.

Josh yelled, "Korbo!" and ran out onto the balcony. But the giant creature was flying off with its prey.

Sickened, Josh turned away. "I was hoping that we could help him."

"I guess he had just gone too far in the dark arts," Sarah said. She put her hand on Josh's arm. "You did your best, Josh. He just didn't want help."

"Thanks, Sarah. But now," he said, "we've got to help his people."

"That's right," she agreed. "They've been under tyranny for so long that they won't know what to do with freedom."

"At least they'll have a chance now," Abbey put in.

"Yeah," Reb said. "All they need is some leadership. This is a good land."

Josh was encouraged by their remarks. "We'll do the best we can," he said. "Let's get started."

16
The Election

Josh and the Sleepers found it more difficult to set right the land than they had supposed. Day after day passed, and the people seemed pathetically helpless. Chief Canto and the chiefs of other villages would meet from time to time, but their villages were really isolated from one another. Each one was a small world, so that they did not know each other well enough to work together.

"I don't know what we're going to do!" Josh finally declared. "How are we going to get them all together?"

The Sleepers were gathered about a table in Chief Canto's house. Gus sat beside Meta. So far, both had been listening but without joining the discussion.

"Well, first we've got to rid the land of these awful beasts," Sarah said.

"We're working on that," Gus said. "We'll have them rooted out soon—if they don't kill us first, of course."

"You've done a good job, Gus," Josh said warmly.

Indeed Gus had. He'd made himself responsible for leading the villagers in hunting down the beasts that Korbo had created. He had been a very busy man indeed and by now seemed to know everybody in every village. "Just give us a few more days, and we'll have the experimental animals taken care of. If they don't rise up against us, of course."

"You've done a wonderful job," Meta said.

"Yes, I have, haven't I?" Gus said with satisfaction. "What other problems do we have? I'm available."

129

Josh laughed. "Well, once we get rid of all the beasts, it seems the big problem is getting these people to get along with each other."

"Why, I think they get along fine," Gus said with amazement. "What makes you think different?"

"They get along fine within their own villages, but the villages need to work with each other. There are some things that take a lot of people to do, not just one village."

"That's right," Dave agreed, "and they're sure not good at that."

"I think," Abbey said slowly, "it's because all their lives they've been cooped up in their own little villages and not really able to get close to anybody else."

"You're right on," Wash said, nodding. He was eating a pear rather noisily and now offered one to Reb. "What they need is some kind of political system."

Dave groaned. "I hate politics."

"Well, you have to have somebody to tie things together. Think how it is with us. We're just a small group, but even *we* need a leader. That's why we have Josh."

Josh felt very good about this. He had now become convinced that his failure was behind him and that he had learned from it. As a matter of fact, he had told Sarah, "I think I can take it now if I *don't* succeed every time I try something."

One day Gus went along with Josh to report to Chief Canto and the other village leaders who had gathered. They all seemed willing enough to listen, but Canto said, "My people trust me, and in the other villages they trust their chief. But no one knows the people in other places, and they don't know us. How can we work together?"

"Maybe we could have an election," Gus said.

"What is an *election?*"

"Oh, I've been listening to some of Reb's stories. He said that back in Oldworld the people in some countries would just get together and choose who was going to rule them."

"I never heard of anything like that," Chief Canto replied, astonished.

"It worked well in some countries," Josh said. "Other countries had kings. That worked pretty well for some, too."

"As for myself, I would prefer not to be ruled by a king. We have heard about kings. Some can become very cruel."

"Well, they can. Others are very kind and love their people, but the people don't have any say in their government."

Canto and his fellow chiefs whispered for a while. Then he turned back to Gus and Josh and said, "We want to have an election."

Gus took great interest in the election proceedings. He had never seen an election and knew nothing about democracy or about governing. He spent a great deal of time listening to the Sleepers explain all this. Then he volunteered to go from village to village, explaining to the people. The villagers seemed to enjoy his poetry about elections, which he made up on the spot. After just a few weeks, he came back to Josh and said, "Well, we're ready for the election."

"So soon?"

"I've talked to every chief, and I've talked to all the people in every village. They're ready to make a choice."

"That's great, Gus. You're a smart fellow."

131

"Yes, I am," Gus said contentedly. "When do you want to have the election?"

"As soon as you can get everybody together."

Election day came a week later. Josh stared at the enormous crowd gathered in the castle courtyard. "They can't all get inside," he said, frowning.

"No," Gus said, "but we can go outside and get their vote."

Josh ordered a raised platform to be built in the courtyard. Then he stepped up on it and lifted his hand for silence.

When all was quiet, he said, "What you are doing here today is deciding on one individual who will help you in every way he can. He will talk to all the chiefs and serve as their counselor. They will bring him their problems, and he will do his best to help solve them."

He made quite a long speech, explaining how democracy worked.

Finally Chief Canto stepped up onto the platform. He said, "It is enough. We understand. Let us have the election."

"All right." Josh grinned. "I *was* being a little long-winded. Now, give me the names of your candidates."

"What is this 'candidate'?" Canto asked in a bewildered way.

"I mean, give me a list of all the men or women that you want to vote on. The one who gets the most votes will be your leader."

"Oh." Canto turned to the crowd. "Who do you want to lead us?"

Everyone began yelling at once.

Josh was half-deafened.

"What are they saying?" Sarah shouted up to him.

"I don't know, but I think they're saying *'Gus'*!"

"They want *Gus* to be their ruler?" Wash said, looking stunned. "I can't believe it!"

Reb grinned. "*He'll* believe it. Wait and see."

Josh walked to the edge of the platform and said, "Gus, come up here."

Gus came up at once, a contented smile on his face.

"Do you want to name another candidate?" Josh asked the people.

"No! We want Gus!" the shout came.

"Do all of you want Gus?"

"Yes! Yes!" everyone shouted. "We want Gus to be our leader!"

Josh Adams could not help laughing. He turned to Gus and said, "You're the best politician I ever saw in my life."

"Well, I like to think they want me not just because I'm the handsomest one in the country but because I'll do a good job. Which I will, of course."

"I believe you will, Gus."

"What will my title be? I can't be a king. People don't like the sound of that word."

"I think we'll call you the *governor*," Josh said, grinning. "Will that sound all right?"

"The governor," Gus said. "Yes. That sounds good. Governor Gustavian Devolutarian."

And so it was that Gus became governor of all the land. He had won the hearts of the people, and everyone seemed happy with their choice. Gus asked if he could make a short speech.

"I will do the best I can for you," he said, "but there is one problem."

"What's that?" Josh asked as the people stood waiting.

"Well, a single man is rather unsteady . . ." Gus seemed to be suddenly at a loss for words.

Josh prompted him. "Then perhaps you ought to get married, Gus."

"What a fine idea!" He looked down at Meta and said to her, "This is a hard thing to ask a young woman. You know how crazy women are about me. There will always be some chasing after me. Can't help that. But if you could put up with that, I think I'd be a good husband."

It appeared that Meta had already seen through Gus and had decided she could put up with him. She came up onto the platform and stood beside the new governor, and all the people cheered.

A huge crowd gathered to watch the Sleepers depart.

"I'm going to miss you, Susie." Josh was holding the baby girl that had been his special charge. He kissed her and then handed her back to her mother. "I'll come back and see her when she's grown."

Sarah said, "I think I'm going to cry," for she had just said good-bye to her own special infant. She turned and walked away.

Before mounting his unicorn, Josh went over to shake hands with Gus. "Gus," he said, "you're a fine fellow. You'll make the best governor in the whole world."

"Or anywhere else for that matter." Gus winked. "Come back and see us, Josh. We need to hear more about Goél."

"I'm sure we'll be coming back, and you'll do fine."

Josh climbed onto the back of his unicorn, then said, "Let's head 'em out."

The Seven Sleepers rode out of the castle walls

and made their way down the road. Everything was green, and flowers bloomed along the roadside.

"It's a different place without those monsters and that crazy magician," Reb said, riding beside him. "Goél sure knows how to put us in the right place at the right time."

On the other side of Josh, Sarah just listened to the two of them talk. She still looked sad at having to leave all the babies.

"I reckon it was a good experience," Reb finally said, summing up everything.

"Reb, is changing diapers harder than killing dragons?" Josh asked suddenly. He winked over at Sarah.

Reb Jackson took off his hat, studied it, then put it back on his head. "I reckon," he said firmly, "I like both. A man needs a little variety!"

Get swept away in the many Gilbert Morris Adventures available from Moody Press:

"Too Smart" Jones

4025-8 Pool Party Thief
4026-6 Buried Jewels
4027-4 Disappearing Dogs
4028-2 Dangerous Woman
4029-0 Stranger in the Cave
4030-4 Cat's Secret
4031-2 Stolen Bicycle
4032-0 Wilderness Mystery

Come along for the adventures and mysteries Juliet "Too Smart" Jones always manages to find. She and her other homeschool friends solve these great adventures and learn biblical truths along the way. Ages 9-14

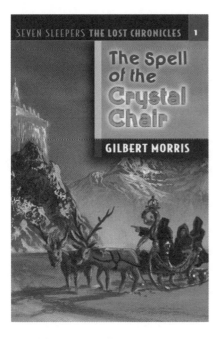

**Seven Sleepers -
The Lost Chronicles**

3667-6 The Spell of the Crystal Chair
3668-4 The Savage Game of Lord Zarak
3669-2 The Strange Creatures of Dr. Korbo
3670-6 City of the Cyborgs

More exciting adventures from the Seven Sleepers. As these exciting young people attempt to faithfully follow Goél, they learn important moral and spiritual lessons. Come along with them as they encounter danger, intrigue, and mystery. Ages 10-14

Dixie Morris Animal Adventures

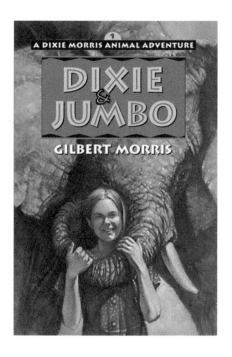

Follow the exciting adventures of this animal lover as she learns more of God and His character through her many adventures underneath the Big Top. Ages 9-14

The Daystar Voyages

Join the crew of the Daystar as they traverse the wide expanse of space. Adventure and danger abound, but they learn time and again that God is truly the Master of the Universe. Ages 10-14

Seven Sleepers Series

3681-1 Flight of the Eagles
3682-X The Gates of Neptune
3683-3 The Swords of Camelot
3684-6 The Caves That Time Forgot
3685-4 Winged Riders of the Desert
3686-2 Empress of the Underworld
3687-0 Voyage of the Dolphin
3691-9 Attack of the Amazons
3692-7 Escape with the Dream Maker
3693-5 The Final Kingdom

Go with Josh and his friends as they are sent by Goél, their spiritual leader, on dangerous and challenging voyages to conquer the forces of darkness in the new world. Ages 10-14

Bonnets and Bugles Series

0911-3 Drummer Boy at Bull Run
0912-1 Yankee Bells in Dixie
0913-X The Secret of Richmond
        Manor
0914-8 The Soldier Boy's Discovery
0915-6 Blockade Runner
0916-4 The Gallant Boys of
        Gettysburg
0917-2 The Battle of Lookout
        Mountain
0918-0 Encounter at Cold Harbor
0919-9 Fire Over Atlanta
0920-2 Bring the Boys Home

Follow good friends Leah Carter and Jeff Majors as they experience danger, intrigue, compassion, and love in these civil war adventures. Ages 10-14